THE DIRTY TURBAN

MICHAEL LEIGHTON

PENNINGTON PUBLISHERS

PENNINGTON PUBLISHERS

ISBN: 978-0-976089-82-7

Trade Paperback (also available on Kindle)

Copyright © 2012 Michael Leighton

All Rights Reserved

Visit us on the Internet at:

web.mac.com/mkleighton

Pennington and the Pennington PP Logo are imprints of Pennington Publishers

Cover design, Interior composition and prepress by:

Donald Brennan for Pennington Publishers / Muse House Press / YakRider Media

Printed in the United States of America

First printing

DEDICATION

When I set out to write this book I had no idea what I was in for. I had written hundreds of magazine articles, but I had never written fiction before. I have never had more fun writing anything.

Producing a novel is a long process and I need to thank my friend Jim Gardner (*The Lion Killer / The Zambezi Vendetta*) who pushed me every step of the way to continue to refine the story, edit the story, and refine it some more. He is a talented author and has been a true inspiration and a great coach to me.

Many of the characters in my book are based on real people, whom I know. Because of this, they must remain unnamed. They know who they are and they should know just how much I appreciated their encouragement and the use of their character in telling my story.

As the book evolved, it became clear that in my own way, I was trying to make a point. The country we live in and the lives we enjoy come to us at a price to someone.

I want to dedicate this book to the uniformed men and women who lost their lives on September 11th, 2001. I had family members who were steel workers on the World Trade Center and I remember when they built it. It tore at my heart to watch it come down like that. The cops and firefighters who ran into that building trying to save the lives of those inside, knew the risks. They went anyway. And to men like Randy Shughart and Gary Gordon, John Wayne Walding and Kent G. Solheim. I never met any of them, but it is apparent to me that my life is what it is because there are people like these willing to do what is necessary, and answer the call. Their individual stories are nothing less than selfless. They represent the attitude, the essence of what it is to be a patriot.

They embody the spirit that makes this country great. They all serve as an inspiration to those who take the time to look for it. To be willing to give so much for an ideal, a principle, a non-tangible, is to me, nothing short of amazing.

ABBOTTABAD, Pakistan, 2 May —
0100 Local Time

On this moonless night members of the US Naval Special Operations Development Group (DEVGRU -SEAL Team Six) and the 160th Special Operations Aviation Regiment (Airborne) under the command of the US Central Intelligence Agency, stormed a 3-story domestic compound in a raid that killed the world's Most Wanted terrorist leader.

A member of SEAL Team Six took out Osama Bin Laden, ending a manhunt that lasted more than a decade and cost thousands of innocent lives.

Despite losing its leader, the al Qaeda organization did not lose their fierce, hate-filled rhetoric, nor the energy behind their malicious determination to destroy America. Enraged, they vowed to retaliate against the United States in any way they can.

In his televised address immediately after the operation, the American president who ordered the raid offered this solemn warning,

"The death of bin Laden marks the most significant achievement to date in our nation's effort to defeat al Qaeda.

Yet his death does not mark the end of our effort. There's no doubt that al Qaeda will continue to pursue attacks against us. We must –- and we will -- remain vigilant at home and abroad".

Yes, they will find and try new ways to hurt us...and their attempts at harming us may become very, *very* personal...

CHAPTER ONE

The van crashed through the barricade. As it accelerated through the crowded parking lot, people scattered. Bob recognized the two men laughing inside. In horror, he watched the vehicle take aim at the stadium gate. The game just ended, and 60,000 football fans moved toward their vehicles.

Unable to move or make a sound, he strained to warn the crowd. As if in slow motion, he watched the speeding vehicle impact the stadium and erupt in a massive fireball. Bob sat helpless, as the maelstrom unfolded. The building collapsed in a choreographed sequence. Bodies and construction debris rained down all around him. The screams of the injured drowned out the roar of the collapsing stadium.

As an armless man ran past, anger and frustration welled inside Bob, followed by an overwhelming sense of resignation. He was powerless.

"Boss?"

A voice cut through the chaos.

"Boss, it's after two."

Bob awoke, finding he fell asleep at his desk. "Wow. I must've dozed off." He wiped sweat off his brow with his sleeve.

"Must have. Everyone's gone, and I'm leaving. See ya tomorrow."

"Good night," Bob said, still groggy.

He went to the washroom, but dousing his face with cold water didn't help. He was still sweating. It was time to go home.

Bob gathered his things and walked outside, where wind blew through him as if he weren't there. "Global warming, my ass," he mumbled.

It was a nasty night on the New Jersey Shore. A raging nor'easter blew up an ice storm with winds over fifty miles per hour. Ice pelted his head and clung to his beard, as he struggled with the padlock. His hip and ankle ached with the cold. The metal pins that held those joints together attracted cold like a magnet, absorbing and storing it before releasing it into his body as pain.

He wrestled the heavy steel gate into position, secured it with a firm tug, then turned toward his car and glanced at his watch. He was on time, but he was *always* on time. Despite his punctuality, the weather promised a long ride home.

As he unlocked his aging sport-utility vehicle, he glanced over his shoulder at the red neon sign hanging over the bar. He fought for the right to display that sign all the way to the State Supreme Court. He needed to know it was on, beckoning those men who might be looking for him. It was his personal expression of how he saw the world.

His twenty-two years in law enforcement left him with a point of view that could be appreciated only by those who sacrificed all in defense of the law and the country. They defended what was right, even when society morphed into political incorrectness. Bob was many things, but politically correct wasn't one of them.

The sign was his way of saying, "Hey! Here I am!" It was also his way of saying, "Thank you for shoving the Constitution up my nose. By the way, since we're on the subject of Constitutional rights, I want to exercise my right to free speech."

"Shit!" he snapped, finding the door lock frozen with ice. He drove his old truck like a badge of honor. Its 170,000 miles became a source of pride to him. He could afford a different vehicle, but it was just another expression of his personal philosophy. *If it works, don't fix it.*

Rummaging through a pocket of his parka, he extracted a lock deicer. Pulling off one glove with his teeth, he shook the cylinder and inserted the tip into the lock. The alcohol-based deicer discharged its contents, spilling onto his fingers and burning him.

The sound of the wind and the sting of the cold reminded him of a time early in his career. On that night many years earlier, he found himself hanging out of a National Guard helicopter in the middle of a blizzard, trying to save a woman in labor. It wasn't going well. He got frostbite on two fingers, the same fingers that currently felt as if they were on fire, but he didn't care. The woman and her baby were fine.

At the time of the incident, he never thought a minor injury would cause pain thirty years later. In the line of duty, one made the choice to sacrifice, a decision made in the moment, with no consideration for long-term consequences. That was how he lived his life every day, and it was also how he managed his career.

That was how he ended up owning a bar on the Jersey Shore, boldly named *The Dirty Turban.* He chose the name, because it was the most-offensive name for which he could get a permit. His choice wasn't driven by bitterness, resentment, or hate. He chose it out of defiance and paid for it with his career.

As snow pummeled his face, he climbed into the aging truck and started the engine. Glancing up at the sign through the fog on his glasses, he saw one letter flickering, and he made a mental note to have it fixed.

Perhaps tonight will be the night, he thought with a smile. *Maybe tonight they will choose to fulfill the promise they broadcast to the entire world on Al Jazeera to rid the world of this infidel.*

His smile wasn't for the sign but for the chance to finish a chapter in his life. He didn't like leaving things unresolved. He needed closure. Drawing a pistol from its holster, he set it in the cup holder between the seats. If they tried tonight, it would be fitting.

As he drove down the street, he marveled at the orange glow of the mercury-vapor streetlights reflected on icicles. The deserted streets looked more like a set from an apocalypse movie than a seaside vacation town.

As he merged onto the Parkway, he approached *the spot.* Only rare individuals were able to look at their lives and identify the exact moment in time or at a specific place where life took a distinct turn. It wasn't like having an accident or being diagnosed with a fatal disease. It was more subtle, a point in time when life took an unforeseen turn, and suddenly, the plan was drastically altered. Bob knew when and where it happened, and he called it *the spot.*

It was just a mile marker on the road, yet four years ago to the day, on a night like this one, everything changed.

Four years earlier, Bob was a captain in the state police and a shoe-in for colonel. On that fateful night, he approached *the spot* in full uniform, driving a state police cruiser, and saw a rental van on the side of the road. Two Middle Eastern-looking men were changing a tire, a fairly common sight on the Parkway. As he approached the truck, his senses went into automatic observation mode.

The truck, a plain-Jane box back, bore the name of a Philadelphia rental company. Its dual rear wheels sat low, as if the truck were heavily loaded. One man was on a cell phone, pacing, while the other struggled with the lug nuts of the defective tire.

Captain Robert Mallory Hershey did what twenty-two years of training and a lifetime of instincts taught him. When he discovered two fifty-five-gallon drums of diesel fuel and two dozen bags of ammonium nitrate in the back of the truck, he knew exactly what was going on. A fifth-grader would have been able to recognize the situation.

After the incident, Captain Hershey was a national hero and overnight media darling. Had the traffic stop occurred a month earlier and under the previous administration's watch, the two men would have won an all-expenses-paid vacation in Guantanamo Bay. The incoming administration, along with the new attorney general, wanted to send a message and used that incident to send it.

After a drawn-out public trial and many televised Congressional hearings, the judge decided that the traffic stop and subsequent search were illegal. The Captain was guilty of racial profiling. The two men driving the truck of explosives were deported to their home country, Pakistan, where they were greeted with the same enthusiasm the Apollo astronauts received upon returning from the moon. The Arabic-language media had its first pair of heroes, two Muslim extremists who beat the infidels at their own game and used their own laws against them.

Hershey was forced to resign or face criminal charges. The State Department hoped he would quickly disappear and his fifteen minutes of fame would pass.

Vindication bore a horrific price. The same two men returned one year later and rented another truck, filled it with fertilizer and diesel fuel, and drove to the parking lot at Giant's Stadium. They may have been the most-popular terrorists on earth, but they were also the most inept.

While attempting to detonate their bomb, they screwed it up and killed only themselves. Bob was immediately contacted by the press. In a live TV interview, he trashed the men, their misguided faith, and those who followed it. His colorful language and less-than-politically correct verbiage were echoed by the New York sports fans that were the intended targets. Though speaking to the press was a clear violation of his agreement to keep his pension, Bob felt he had nothing to lose.

That interview, and subsequent interviews with *The New York Times* and *The Washington Post*, placed a target on his back, and that was how he liked it. Bob felt his nation had lost its way. He believed the lessons of 9/11 were lost. He opined that in the pursuit of perpetrators of terror, domestic or foreign, all was fair and good. In his opinion, what happened at *the spot* represented all that was wrong with American politics.

As he drove past *the spot*, his peace was broken by his ringing cell phone.

"Hey, Dude." He tried to mask his exhaustion by using his favorite universal adjective.

"Don't Dude me. I'm just checking on ya," the voice replied.

"I appreciate it. It's been a long day, I'm headed home, and the weather sucks. But at least I'm not flyin' in it." he taunted his caller.

"Me, neither, Bro. My flying-in-shit-weather days are over. I knew you'd be headed home about now, and I was just checking in, it being the anniversary and all...." His voice faded.

"I'm fine, just tired. I'll be down your way in about a week. We'll do lunch." He wanted to end the conversation.

"Cool, Man. See ya then. You know where to find me. Say hi to the wife for me."

"Will do." Bob pressed the *Call End* button.

The caller was Keith Michaels, one of only three people on earth Bob trusted.

Michaels set down the phone on the nightstand and reached for the light switch. Deborah, his wife, lifted her head from the pillow and squinted into the light.

"Who are you talking to at two in the morning?" she asked.

"Bob. I was just checking on him."

"Everything all right?"

"Yeah."

Michaels and Bob met a lifetime earlier, two men thrust into a situation that bound them in friendship for life. They met on a bridge in the Philippines at the entrance to the Subic Bay Naval Base. The bridge spanned the Shit River, so named for the volume of raw sewage that ran under it from the city of Olongapo. Bob was part of a Military Police unit, while Michaels was a second lieutenant in the Air Force.

Also on the bridge that night was Marine Gunnery Sergeant Brian Pysinski, a first-generation immigrant whose family escaped Communism and immigrated to Cleveland.

Coincidence placed them on the bridge that particular evening. Warrant Officer Hershey had a twenty-four-hour pass. He joined the Army to put distance between himself and his namesake. He pronounced his name *Her-see* in an attempt to separate himself from his famous family name. He was after all, a Hershey, like the famous chocolate bar.

Bob was a major disappointment to his family, because he had no interest in the family business. All he wanted to be his entire life was a cop. His father nearly had a heart attack at the thought of his son doing "that kind or work."

To buy time and gain experience, he joined the Army and then the Military Police. He was on his first deployment. Built like a professional wrestler, he could have gotten a scholarship to play college football, but the Hershey's didn't play football. They were more suited to sports like Polo. Bob would have needed to ride a Clydesdale to support his massive frame.

Pysinski was on his way home after twelve months of keeping South Korea safe from North Korea. The completion of his uneventful twelve-month tour earned him a coveted drill-instructor slot on Parris Island.

Michaels was escorting a B-52 loaded with nuclear warheads home from South Korea. The plane had a mechanical problem and landed at Clark Air Force Base for repairs. Michaels went with the nukes. He was really a glorified atomic baby-sitter. Senior officers called him Nukem, pronounced Newcomb. None of that was in the brochure when he saw a recruiter during his senior year of high school. Michaels' timing sucked.

He graduated from high school in the spring of 1976. Saigon fell in September, 1975, and the Armed Forces of the United States of America was in the middle of the biggest downsizing since VJ Day. Strategic Air Command was one of the few areas of the military that wasn't having funding problems. The Cold War was on.

Michaels needed to attend college, but the military had just transitioned to an all-volunteer force. He got his four years of college, but, when it came time for a military operations specification decision, he faced his current job or becoming part of a missile-silo crew. Spending six years at the bottom of a 400-foot-deep hole somewhere in Kansas, waiting for the President to call so he could turn a key and end the world, didn't have many civilian-world applications.

The President would never trust one man to end the world, so both soldiers were issued guns—in case the other guy refused to turn the key when instructed. Then it was the first man's job to shoot his partner and turn his key, too.

He chose to be an atomic bomb sitter instead. At least he wasn't stuck in a hole in Kansas, and he got to fly *in* an airplane. What he always wanted was to be a pilot. He'd been a pilot since he was a teenager and was fully qualified. As a kid, he rode his bike to the airport and washed planes all day for a chance at a ride. He soloed on his sixteenth birthday and got his license on his seventeenth. But in the post-Vietnam era military, the only way to get a flying billet in any of the armed services was to go to one of the academies, which required a Congressional appointment, something Jewish kids from New York never got.

Thus fate placed him, Hershey, and Pysinski, along with twenty others, on that bridge. The air was heavy with the odor of human waste. Faint streetlights barely illuminated the river's surface. The distant sound of jets taking off and landing, the constant jabber of a foreign language, and the incessant peeping of dozens of ducklings in a bamboo cage cast a surreal scene.

They were engaged in a form of gambling. For entertainment, locals tossed baby ducklings into the river, and the crocodiles knew it. The last duck remaining was the winner. The ducks were numbered, and members of the crowd bet on his duck as if it were a horse in a race. The practice was sick and depraved, but it was all there was for entertainment for those not interested in drinking or spending the night with a prostitute in Olongapo.

Bloop!

Another duckling vanished below the surface, and the deranged crowd cheered.

"Oh, Man, that's just not right," Pysinski said to no one in particular.

Trying to contain his nervous laughter, Michaels replied, "Yeah. I'm glad they sent us here to defend these people's freedom and preserve their right to a quality lifestyle."

Hershey turned. "Hey, Air Force. Double or nothing on number three."

"No way, Man. I won't bet money on a friggin' duck," he said over his laughter.

"OK. The loser buys the drinks for the night."

"Can I get in on that?" Pysinski asked.

"Sure. What about it, Lieutenant?" Hershey's sarcastic, drawn-out emphasis on the word *Lieutenant* made Michaels pause.

Looking the MP in the eye, Michaels saw a well-practiced poker face.

"Come on, three!"

Bloop!

The crowd sighed.

"Two! Two! Two!" the crowd chanted.

Bloop! Only two ducklings remained.

Bloop!

"Oh, no."

"You win, Mr. Hershey." Congratulations came with the

same sarcastic emphasis on *Mister* he got from Hershey. He knew how Army warrant officers were sensitive to that title.

Hershey looked at Michaels, who waited. After an uncomfortable, pregnant pause, one that might be followed by a handshake or a right cross, Hershey smiled and turned toward town. "Come on, Lieutenant. You're buying."

"Come on, Gunny," Michaels told the Marine. "You wanted in, so you're in."

The three men walked toward town.

Michaels was a terrible drunk. His 175-pound frame was incapable of handling alcohol in any quantity. Pysinski and Hershey drank like it was an Olympic event, and Michaels was a good sport. He lost fair and square, and he didn't have anything better to do than hang out with two strangers and watch them drink away his money. It was more entertaining than watching ducklings disappear into the Shit River.

A few hours, a few laughs, and a few fifths of Johnny Walker later, the three agreed to call it a night. As they stumbled out of the bar, they were greeted by an armed Shore Patrol and local police.

The United States military wasn't particularly welcome in the Philippines. Like Americans, Filipinos had short memories. They forgot that, if it weren't for the Armed Forces of the U.S., their entire nation would be speaking Japanese. It didn't matter that the U.S. military complex was the largest source of employment on the island and the engine that drove the economy. Negotiations of leases for the bases at Clark and Subic Bay were up for renewal, and that was a sensitive political issue for the Department of Defense.

The local radical anti-American group hatched a plan to create animosity toward the American military during negotiations for the bases. A local girl claimed she was raped, and the perpetrators were reported to be three American servicemen. Hershey, Michaels, and Pysinski fit the description.

After a long night, the three men woke in the brig at Subic Bay. The Naval Criminal Investigative Service and the Judge Advocate General's office cut a deal with the locals to handle the problem. It became a media and public-relations spectacle. The men were separated, and investigators tried to get one to turn against the others for two days. On day three, despite consistent stories from all three men, patience and tempers wore thin.

Michaels sat in the same Interrogation room for sixteen grueling hours, and the New Yorker in him began to show. He desperately wanted a shower and a cup of coffee. Trying to drive a wedge between the three men was the Navy's top interrogator, Captain Steven Kirk. He stood just five-foot-six-inches tall with sandy hair and a baby face. Only a bad hair dye job betrayed his advanced age. At forty-six, he was still a captain.

"Good morning, Lieutenant." He walked into the room with his Shore Patrol guard and placed his briefcase on the gray steel mil-spec table that separated him from Michaels. "I'm Captain Kirk."

Michaels couldn't control his laughter. Tears soon ran down his face. "Captain Kirk? Does that make me...Mr. Spock?" He continued laughing.

"I'm not amused by Captain Kirk jokes, Lieutenant."

"Are you here to fly around Uranus and look for Klingons?"

Leaning across the table, the Captain spoke sternly using the same tone one would use with a dog that just crapped on the carpet. "Listen up, Lieutenant. Just because you're in the brig doesn't mean I can't charge you with insubordination."

"I think I understand." Michaels stopped laughing, stood, and glared at the Captain. "As opposed to a jacked-up charge of rape?" He knew it was a rhetorical question. "Now *you* listen up, Captain."

Michaels lowered his voice and leaned across the table until he was inches from the captain's face. "I've had about as much fun as I can stand. I don't know what the deal is here, but whatever it is, it wasn't us. I just met those guys the night we were picked up. We walked into town and had a few drinks. We were arrested as we left the bar.

"I'm not gonna tell ya they did it, because I know they didn't. They won't tell you I did it, because I didn't. Maybe that's not what you want to hear, but that's the deal."

Michaels straightened. "I've asked for a lawyer more than once. When someone tells me what the hell's going on here, then we can proceed. That's what I told the other investigators. I'm tired of repeating it. Until then, Sir, I have nothing more to add."

He sat and stared at the Captain.

Without speaking, Kirk picked up his case, turned toward the door, took a step, and stopped. Still facing away from Michaels, he said, "For the record, that's exactly what the other two said, including the part about the Klingons."

He strutted from the room without looking back. His Shore Patrol guard escort closed the door behind him.

Michaels sat there stunned, not sure what to make of the encounter. He was only certain of being tired. He'd slept only four hours in the last two days.

A few minutes later, Kirk returned with a Styrofoam cup in each hand. The guard wasn't with him. He kicked the door closed with his foot, placed the cups on the table, and turned a chair around before sitting to face Michaels.

The room was totally silent.

"Look, Captain. I'm sorry about the Klingon cracks. I'm just exhausted," Michaels admitted.

"Save it, Lieutenant. In a minute, I'll have Pysinski and Hershey brought in. I'll explain this only once."

"Explain what?"

"You'll get it in a minute, Lieutenant." Kirk's teeth clenched.

Michaels, hearing footsteps coming down the hall, recognized the sound of several men walking in loose formation. The door flew open, and in walked Hershey and Pysinski, accompanied by armed guards. Both men looked exhausted.

"Could you get us a couple more chairs?" Kirk asked the guard.

A few seconds later, a guard returned with two military-issue gray steel chairs and placed them near the table.

"Please sit, Gentlemen," Kirk said.

"Now we're gentlemen?" quipped Pysinski.

"Sit down, Gunny." Kirk rolled his eyes.

"Aye, Captain." Pysinski used his best Mr. Scott accent.

Kirk rolled his eyes again. Hershey sat silently, arms crossed, chin slightly down, eyes moving from one man to the next. His jaw muscles tensed and relaxed, as he struggled to control himself.

"In a few minutes," Kirk began, "a Rear Admiral from the Judge Advocate General's office will walk in here. He'll tell you the incident in which you've been implicated has international repercussions. He'll also tell you the Department of Defense wants it to go away, and that includes you three. "

"What the fuck?" Pysinski chirped.

"Don't speak, Gunny. Just listen." Kirk raised his index finger to the young Marine but continued staring at Hershey. "You men happened to be in the wrong place at the wrong time. You're collateral damage in a political battle. You understand the concept of collateral damage?"

Without waiting for an answer, he continued, "I'm not the bad guy here. You don't have to heed my advice. I'm speaking to you off the record, not as an officer in the United States military. Is that clear? Take the Admiral's words very seriously, and take his offer when he makes it. Shut up and go home. It's that simple."

"Captain?" Hershey spoke. "Are we still off the record?"

"Yes."

"Then exactly what the fuck's going on here? In English, please, so a stupid warrant officer can understand."

Kirk paused and looked around as if preparing to tell a racist joke, then said softly, "This has to do with derailing the base lease negotiations. The offer you will receive comes all the way from the

White House. Please, Gentlemen, don't fuck this up."

The door opened, and a guard entered the room. "Attention on deck!"

Everyone stood. A moment later, Rear Admiral Winston Chester MacAfee stepped into the room. In his mid-fifties and a career officer, he knew a shit deal when he saw one, but it was his job to sell this one. "At ease, Gentlemen. Please be seated. I'll be brief. I just flew in from Honolulu to speak with you. I suspect Captain Kirk has filled you in on some of the details."

Even the admiral couldn't say "Captain Kirk" without smiling. "I've been authorized to offer the three of you the opportunity to accept an honorable discharge from your respective services and transportation stateside, effective immediately, with one caveat. You must sign a nondisclosure agreement and may never discuss any of the terms or conditions, the conditions of your arrest, or anything else surrounding this event. That means you can't tell anyone, not even your wife, girlfriend, or mother. Is that clear?"

"Do we get a minute to think about it?" Michaels asked.

The admiral turned to his entourage. "Gentlemen, may I have the room, please?" It was an order disguised as a request.

A moment later, they were alone.

"Off the record?"

"Yes, Sir."

"I know this is a shit deal. I hope none of you planned to become career officers. This is a national security issue. The president doesn't want the scandal to affect the lease negotiations. In a few weeks, long after you're home and mustered out, the JAG office will give a press release stating that no credible evidence of the charge was found. Your names won't be released to the press. It will get swept under the rug, and you three will remain anonymous."

"Any other option?" Michaels pressed.

"Lieutenant, the other option is I find you guilty and sentence all of you to hard labor in Leavenworth for twenty years. How's that sound, Soldier?"

"But you know we didn't do it!" Pysinski said.

"It doesn't matter what I know. This is a public-relations clusterfuck, and you're in the middle of it. We had the same shit happen in Panama, except that time, we ended up giving the damn canal back to them. Do you three assholes want to be the reason we lose our forward base in the Southeast Pacific? I don't think so. I will open the door now, and when the Captain returns, we sign the deal and all go home. Agreed?"

They nodded silently.

Forty-eight hours later, the three men were on a transport to Honolulu headed toward home. It wasn't a comfortable ride. The passenger area on the Star Lifter was noisy and cold. The plane wasn't made for hauling people, so accommodations were cattle class.

Nine hours on the flight, followed by an eleven-hour jaunt to Dobbins Air Force Base, gave the men time to accept the hand fate dealt them. More importantly, they had time to vent and bond. It was heavy stuff for a couple of twenty-somethings far from home and all alone.

As dissimilar as the men were, they also had remarkable similarities. All three went on to marry and stayed married for more than twenty years. All were driven to careers they dreamed about as kids. They were fiercely loyal men, a quality they found in each other. It would have been easy to file a false statement against one of them. Unfortunately for the JAG, none of them was willing to turn in the others to save himself.

They met as strangers on a bridge half a world from home. When they parted that final night in Atlanta, they were brothers who dodged a bullet together on the wild ride some called "life experience." Their horrible, nightmarish ordeal became one of the single greatest moments in each man's life. They attended each other's weddings, became godparents of each other's children, and helped guide each other's careers.

Michaels rolled over, reached up, and turned off the light. He was true to his nature. Concerned about his friend, he offered moral support to the buddy who managed to get screwed for political expediency not once but twice in a lifetime, which had to be some sort of record.

Michaels knew few people became close to Bob. Bob had buddies, guys he hunted, golfed, and played cards with, but only four people on earth were close to him, including his wife and himself. That was another similarity between them. Each walked the earth as if alone in a crowd, yet totally content. Only one woman entered each man's personal sphere of influence, and even they had limits, though none of them knew it. It was a solitary emotional existence based on a character trait that allowed mental clarity without distraction, not a lack of emotional capacity. That particular characteristic facilitated monocular focus on command, permitting concentration without emotional "noise."

It was a valuable tool once they learned how to use it. None of the men realized such a time was fast approaching.

CHAPTER TWO

Though it was nearly three AM on the East Coast, it was afternoon in Jalalabad, the terrorist capital of the world after the U.S. government closed the prison at Guantanamo Bay. The politically popular move to close Gitmo left the American administration with a perplexing problem. What should it do with the 200 prisoners housed there? Transporting known terrorist into the States wasn't a popular idea. Senators and members of Congress who supported closing the prison vehemently opposed bringing terrorists into their districts. In the end, the administration decided to return many of the detainees to their host countries, including Khalid Sheikh Mohammed.

Nicknamed KSM by the media, because that was easier than printing his entire name, he was the brains behind the World Trade Center bombing in 1993 and the September 11, 2001, attacks. If brought to the U.S. to stand trial, he would have been transported to New York State, which didn't have a death penalty. If he were tried and convicted, he would be incarcerated in the New York State Correctional System. The cost associated with housing him, as well as the potential for making New York an even-bigger target for terrorists than it already was, compelled the junior senator from New York, turned Secretary of State, to convince Afghanistan to take him back.

Though KSM was born in Kuwait, he spent much of his time in Afghanistan, where he fought against the Soviet invasion and met Osama bin Laden. After Gitmo closed, bin Laden came out of hiding and was reunited with his stalwart lieutenant. They began rebuilding Al-Qaeda and reenergizing the holy war on the West.

Another unintended consequence of the new administration's policies was that Al-Qaeda became emboldened. No longer forced to hide in caves, the members began operating in the open, which terrified the oil-producing nations in the Middle East. Bin Laden could easily put them out of business. That caused an instant power shift in nuclear Pakistan and India, countries already struggling with internal faction fights between the Sunni and Shiite sects.

Al-Qaeda morphed into, for lack of a better description, the Islamic Mafia, with bin Laden as the grandfather, and KSM the enforcer. Instead of paying protection money for a grocery store or flower shop, one paid it for an entire country. Soon, Al-Qaeda sat on billions in untraceable assets in neutral countries and sympathetic banks around the world. No longer did they have to fight with leftover Soviet-era junk. They could afford to buy whatever they wanted.

Bin Laden and KSM deliberately stayed low tech, believing technology could be beaten by better technology, and the U.S. had the best. However, technology was no match for unsophisticated, simple-as-a-rock forms of aggression that were Al-Qaeda's trademark. Bin Laden remained free by using human messengers, not telephones, and handwritten messages, not e-mail. His men used box cutters instead of firearms.

It was an effective strategy. Jalalabad, halfway between Kabul and Peshawar, was the perfect place to practice. It was a lawless, Third-World shithole of a city, flush with poor, illiterate, uneducated Muslim men who were ready to drink extremist Kool-Aid and join the *jihad* against the West. A city devoid of technology, it was the perfect breeding ground for terrorists, a place that time and the rest of the world had long forgotten. The steel-roofed adobe and concrete shacks ran for miles in all directions with no sign of modern sewers, water pipes, or electrical power.

The only sign the dilapidated city was in the twentieth century was the loudspeaker atop the spires of the mosques, calling the faithful to pray. In the middle of that medieval environment, two young men walked hurriedly across the square. Hot dust and midday sun forced them to squint, as they hustled through the crowded streets. The smell of animals permeated the air. Even though it was winter, it was winter in the desert.

Rushi Kumar Ali and Akshay al Kadam were like many other men in that part of the world. Growing up in a place where only the strong survived, they learned to live on the street at a young age, which made them prime candidates to join the Jihadists. Hearing about that struggle since they were little boys, they knew it was the cause their fathers fought and died for.

Rushi and Akshay were cousins. Their fathers were the two men on the side of the road who changed Bob Hershey's life forever.

When they returned to Pakistan, after Hershey foiled their first attempt to become martyrs, they were greeted as heroes. Rushi and Akshay were young, but not too young to appreciate their newfound celebrity. The sons of heroes were the heroes of the future. When their fathers failed to complete their mission, they were regarded as traitors to the cause in Afghanistan. Suddenly, Rushi and Akshay went from being the sons of heroes to the sons of traitors.

They would carry that burden and shame the rest of their lives. The *jihadist* leaders blamed their fathers' failure on the infidel Hershey, who interfered with God's plan. Though the failure was never mentioned aloud, Al-Qaeda offered the two boys a chance at redemption. They could lift the shame from their family names.

They moved hurriedly across the square to the meeting place. They were summoned to the cause, called to meet the man who, with Allah's help, outlasted the infidels' patience, torture, and internment at Guantanamo. They would meet KSM, who was almost a living god in Jalalabad. He was often seen dining in public, moving on the streets in broad daylight, and speaking publicly to the adoring crowds that worshipped him.

The common man didn't speak to KSM. He spoke to them. It was improper even to look him in the eye. Instead, people spoke to his lieutenants and referred to KSM in the third person, as if he was not there.

The boys climbed the stairs to the second floor, taking two steps at a time. When they reached the landing, two men directed them into a flat overlooking the bustling square below.

Hiding in plain sight and surrounded by hundreds of people,

KSM knew he was safe from any kind of high-tech retaliation from the West. Between satellites and remote-piloted vehicles, America and her allies knew where he was, what he ate, and even the kind of watch he wore, but they didn't dare strike at him without risking great collateral damage. Even if they managed to kill him, the political fallout at home would send the American system into self-consumption mode if any civilians died in the process.

For years, whenever the Americans bombed an Al-Qaeda training camp or command center, the surviving members rounded up dozens of innocent civilians, brought them to the site, and killed them. As soon as representatives of the news media arrived, they blamed the Americans for murdering civilians. The strategy worked so well, the Americans completely stopped bombing.

It was dark inside the flat. The shutters were drawn, the curtains closed, except for one small window. The stench of food, animals, and feces hung in the smoky air.

"Do you know why you're here?" The voice came from a figure in the mostly darkened room. KSM sat at a table alone, his bodyguards only two steps away. Two AK-47s leaned against the filthy wall.

Rushi and Akshay went to their knees half a room away.

"Yes, we know," Rushi answered for both of them. His voice cracked, as he bowed his head in reverence.

"Then tell me out loud, so we all may hear." The owner of the voice stepped from the shadows, so the boys could see him clearly. He was six-feet-six-inches tall, fully bearded, and wore a combination of traditional Arab clothes and a military utility vest. At first glance, he looked like a young Osama bin Laden, but there was no way that could be true.

"We're here," Akshay answered, "because we were chosen to honor the *Jihad* and pay death to the infidels who oppose us."

"You're here to defend your families' honor and to play a part in turning the infidels against each other. They're weak. They can be bought, coerced, and compelled to sell each other out for money. They're sentimental fools, who, for the love of a woman, can be made to commit disgraceful acts against their own kind.

"That's the fallacy of the West. You'll prove that to the world. Just as your brothers used their lifestyles against them on that glorious day in September, you shall use their weaknesses against them. You and your cousin were chosen for this long ago. We taught you to read, write, and understand English, so you could complete this mission. Are you ready?"

"Yes, Your Greatness," Rushi said. "We're ready."

"Then get up off your knees. Today you become men. Come to the table."

They rose and walked toward the table. KSM stood without speaking and moved away, allowing the tall one to take his seat. The table was lit by the open window, but the rest of the room was dark. Others were in the room, though they weren't visible. Someone had been smoking opium just before the boys arrived, and the stench hung in the thick air.

"Here's what you must do," the tall one said. "You'll leave here and travel by train to Uzbekistan. From there, you fly via commercial airliner to Sweden and on to Cuba. You'll be supplied with Pakistani passports and visas and will be given five thousand Euros to get you to Havana. When you arrive, you'll go to the Credit Suisse branch office and ask for a manager named Mubarak. Show him this key."

The tall man extended his arm. Fist closed, he opened it to reveal a safety-deposit key on a leather tether. Rotating his hand, he dangled the key on its tether from his thumb. Rushi took it and hung the key around his neck.

"This key is for a safety deposit box in your name. In the box will be everything you need to complete your mission, including money, phones, and further instructions. From there, you'll meet a man whose name and cell phone number are in the box. He'll smuggle you into America.

"Once there, you will kidnap the wife of the infidel Hershey and bring her to us in the Bahamas. We'll be waiting. Once we have her, Hershey will do whatever we want in order to save her. We'll make him complete your fathers' unfinished work. That is your mission. Do you understand?"

The boys nodded in fear and pride.

"I must hear you say it!" He raised his voice and slammed his palm against the table.

The boys jumped back as if shocked by electricity. During a sickening, pregnant pause, a dog yelped in the street. They heard the other men in the room whispering, but they couldn't make out the words. A few feet away, the sound of a gun being cocked reverberated through the hot room.

"Yes, I understand," Rushi replied, keeping his eyes on the

table and not daring to look up. "We won't fail."

There was another pause, and then the door opened into the darkened hall.

"Wait here for five minutes. Don't speak or move. After a few minutes, leave this place and go as you were instructed. Don't fail me. Your families couldn't stand another failure."

The tall one walked toward the door.

Both boys remained motionless, their eyes locked on the table for five minutes, contemplating the threat. If they failed or changed their minds, their families would die. If they succeeded, their families would likely claim a cash reward. Had they hesitated or balked when the tall one gave them their orders, they'd already be dead. That was how Al-Qaeda controlled its recruits.

Without speaking, the boys picked up the money, passports, and train tickets.

Akshay opened the ticket jacket with a shaking hand. "The train leaves tonight."

Rushi took the cell phone from the table and stuffed it into his jacket. They hurried toward the door.

"We must go home, get our things, and say our good-byes," Akshay said.

"No. We tell no one what we're doing."

"But we might never come back."

They froze as the full realization of the situation struck. Simultaneously, they concluded it might be the last time they saw their home, families, or anything else they knew. The ultimate sacrifice for the cause didn't begin with death. It started when one agreed to sacrifice his life for the cause.

"No one can know," Rushi said. "No one."

The train looked like it came from a movie set. Coal- and wood-powered engines from a bygone era provided semireliable locomotion to aging passengers and freight cars. No diesel or electric power was available.

Rushi and Akshay found two seats in an ancient Pullman car and sat with a woman, her three grandchildren, and their goat. The woman looked in her fifties, which was considered old for that part of the world. Sitting in the car, eating a melon, she motioned the boys to sit. Whatever language she spoke, neither of the boys recognized it, so communication was relegated to sign language.

The goat expressed mild curiosity toward them, which made the children laugh. The children were between the ages of five and nine, but they were so malnourished it was difficult to tell.

Rushi and Akshay settled into their seat as the train lurched forward on its long trek through the mountains. The corridor echoed with a cacophony of noise from people who still hadn't found seats. The person acting as conductor moved slowly from car to car, checking tickets. On the platform, uniformed military carrying automatic weapons got little attention from the crowds hustling past.

The old woman held a piece of melon in her hand and offered the boys a bite. Akshay smiled and declined with a wave. He and Rushi were exhausted. The adrenalin they ran on for hours was finally gone. The sun was warm through the window. The smell of burning coal and wood wafted through an open vent. Within minutes, both boys drifted in and out of sleep.

Akshay woke to something brushing his nose. He opened his eyes, forgetting where he was, and saw the car was illuminated by a single tiny blue lightbulb in the ceiling. When he managed to focus his eyes, he was face-to-face with the goat, which was eating the top button of his coat, its whiskers tickling his nose.

Akshay jumped back in surprise. The goat, undeterred, continued pursuing the button. Across the car, the old lady laughed. Her grandchildren sprawled across the seats, their heads resting on her lap, while she continued eating a piece of melon.

Akshay saw the goat had eaten all his buttons but one. He smacked Rushi to wake him.

"What?" Rushi rubbed sleep from his eyes, his mouth glued shut from breathing through it while he slept. "Are we stopping?"

"No. This stupid goat ate all the buttons off my coat."

Rushi took a moment to process that statement. "What did you say?"

"I said the goat ate all the buttons off my coat."

Rushi paused, fighting an impending smile without success. "Then you should kick its ass, shouldn't you? If he gets away and tells the other goats how...how easy it was you'll never get any respect. No goat will ever take you seriously."

"How do they say it in America? Go fuck yourself. Yes. That's it."

Halfway around the world, it was a beautiful morning. Emily Riley Smith-Hershey packed her sea bags. She was an avid and sought-after sailboat captain. Born Emily Riley Smith, she hated her first name, and only her husband used it, though he called her "Em," not Emily. That was their secret code when he wasn't able to talk freely, such as situations when there were people in the room, he was in a patrol car with another officer, or there was another reason. It wasn't a conscious thing but had evolved during twenty years of marriage.

Everyone else called her Riley. For most of her life, she kept her maiden name, partly because, in Bob's line of work, he occasionally made enemies. Sometimes, it was safer not to share his last name. Bob agreed. He never wanted his professional life to affect his family, but some things couldn't be predicted or controlled.

Riley made a name for herself in the sailboat world when she was part of the first all-female crew to compete in the Whitbread Race. Later, she was the first woman to race on an American boat in the America's Cup. She grew up in the Bahamas and sailed with her dad when she was a child. The late seventies and early eighties were fast times in the Bahamas, and her father disappeared one night in an airplane under suspicious circumstances. On the island, people speculated he was involved with the booming drug trade plying the Florida Straits, but she didn't believe it. She never learned what happened to him.

Her last memory of her father occurred the weekend before he disappeared. The two of them went snorkeling near Walkers Cay when they found a gold coin. He called it "their treasure." Together, they buried the treasure in a small metal box on Sandy Cay, an uninhabited spit of land just north of West End. They marked the spot with a pile of stones like pirates did in the movies. It was their little secret, and that was the last time she saw him alive. After her dad disappeared, her family moved to Palm Beach, where she fit right in with the Southern Ocean Racing Conference crowd that wintered on Hobe Sound.

As a teen and in her early twenties, Riley was stunning, with blonde hair, blue eyes, and a husky voice that enabled her to get whatever she wanted. Her Christy Brinkley good looks, perfect body, semipermanent tan, and infectious smile opened any doors she needed. She wasn't stupid, either. With an IQ of 150, she was close to genius.

Emotionally, she felt alone since her dad went missing, so she became skilled in the art of emotional manipulation. Riley would get somewhat close to someone, and, when the feelings became real, she sailed off without looking back. In the pre-cell-phone world, it was easy to disappear, and she often did. On land, she was just another pretty face with a hot body. On the ocean, she was in control of her world. She could read the sea, wind, and tide as easily as some people breathed. On the water, she was close to her dad.

At sixteen, she earned her captain's license. Riley spent her summers on the Cape and winters at her Florida home. It was a great life, hobnobbing with the rich and famous and their sons.

She put herself through college ferrying sailboats north and south between the Cape and Florida, as the seasons changed. Much of that sailing was done single-handedly, a testament to her skill, because it took real seamanship to handle a sixty-foot sailboat alone.

Sailing gave her everything in life that was important, and it was also how she met Bob. He was a young trooper assigned to a detail covering the Americas Cup team trails in Cape May, New Jersey. Riley wanted to make the team. Both were individuals who spent months at a time away from home and who trusted no one but themselves. They always felt alone in a crowd.

As different as they were, they shared a remarkable craving for life. On one of their early dates, Bob took her caribou hunting in Alaska. If she could handle hunting, the rest would be easy. For years, a photo of Riley in full camo sat on his desk.

After that trip, he knew he would marry her. Soon, she accepted the fact that the innocuous, low-key, serious-as-a-heart-attack trooper from New Jersey found a way around her formidable emotional defenses. She learned to shoot, and he learned to sail. She was comfortable in her own skin, whether in camo or a bikini, and Bob was in awe of a woman that beautiful who could out fight and out drink most men.

Approaching fifty, she was stunningly beautiful. The crow's feet at the corners of her eyes didn't detract from her magnetic smile, and her eyes were as clear and bright as when she was a teenager. Her fine, blonde hair showed a few streaks of gray, but she liked the change. Most days, her hair was in a ponytail under a baseball cap. She never wore makeup or high heels except at those dreadful official functions she attended to support Bob's career or at an occasional funeral, fundraiser, or award dinner. Her flirtatious nature allowed men of all ages to hit on her, and she shamelessly enjoyed the attention. It did wonders for her ego, and Bob liked it, too.

Still in tremendous demand as a captain, she commanded $25,000 a month in season to do what she would normally have done for free. Every year for the past fifteen years, Riley headed south to captain a large sailing yacht for a wealthy family throughout the Caribbean. To her, it was like being paid to take a vacation. It certainly wasn't about the money, though she always pointed that out to Bob's family, who didn't approve of her career. It was about being on the sea, close to what she considered home, doing what she loved.

Nor was it roughing it either. These yachts were seventy feet or more and equipped with the latest amenities and technology. She always picked her own crew, including a mate and cook, and personally provisioned the boat. Now, if everything went according to plan, she would put to sea by the end of the week. She wouldn't be home until April, but since Bob stopped working, he could fly down to visit her while she was docked in a port of call for a few days. Last year it was Nevis. The year before, it was Trinidad.

This year, she was leaving early to take care of her personal pride and joy. For her fortieth birthday, Bob bought her dream boat, a forty-two-foot custom sloop built to her personal specifications. That sailboat incorporated everything she learned about sailboat racing and boat handling into a ship she and Bob could sail around the world if they wished. After Bob retired, they planned to sail to Hawaii, Alaska, and the South Pacific.

Bob's retirement came early and unanticipated, so he wasn't mentally ready to drop off the grid so soon. Riley needed to give him space. Though Bob went hunting and fishing and did some occasional contract work for the state law-enforcement divisions, the bar became the emotional epicenter of his life and gave him focus.

Riley was OK with that for the moment. He was surrounded by friends in the bar, because he hired his friends to run it. She knew anyone who hung out at the Turban was at least sympathetic to the situation. A smart woman, she knew forcing him to sail for a year or two would only exacerbate the situation. She waited this long, so another year or two wouldn't matter.

She finished packing her bags, knowing she could buy whatever she forgot, and tossed them down the stairs. Bob had the car warmed up for the ride to the airport. Standing in the middle of the bedroom, she looked around. Whatever she left lying about would be in the exact same place when she returned. It was weird, like putting time on hold, but that's how it was.

She wouldn't miss the miserable cold. In a few hours, she would shed her sweater and boots for a tank top and shorts. The only time she put on shoes was when going ashore. It was an interesting way to live, and, as she was fond of saying, "It does not suck."

"I left my itinerary on the kitchen table, along with the SAT and cell numbers," she said. "We're supposed to put in at Provincial in Turks and Cacaos for about a week, so, if you really miss me, you could come down then." She gave him a puppy-dog stare.

Bob smiled. "We'll see. I mean, it's not like I have anything to do, anyway." He stuck his tongue into the side of his cheek.

They laughed. Bob put the truck in drive and set off toward the airport. "What's the boat you're on this year again?"

She told him five times already and sighed before answering.

"I told you it's Randy and Millie's boat. They had a family who wanted a bare-boat charter, but they wouldn't let it go without me running it. Their renter hired me directly. I'll have Richie and Carol, the same crew as last year."

Bob knew Richie and Carol and felt comfortable. They were good people. "Yeah, yeah, I remember. I was just busting your balls to make you tell me again. You know, it's the same way you ask me what I'm doing and who I'm doing it with over and over."

She punched his bicep.

Bob hesitated, and then asked, "Christ, what was that? It's too friggin' cold for mosquitoes. I think something just bit me."

Riley smiled and muttered, "Jerk." She unsnapped her seat belt and lifted the console between the seats to lie down with her head in his lap like a little kid. They drove silently, listening to the radio, Bob holding the wheel with one hand and stroking her hair with the other. It was a quiet, quality moment spent with a life partner before being parted.

She was asleep before they merged onto the highway. That would be the last time she slept with both eyes shut until she returned at the end of the cruise. Riley learned long ago that the captain was always on duty. Even though her crew, with whom she sailed a dozen times before, we're both skilled seamen, she never really slept while in charge of the boat.

The Dirty Turban

CHAPTER THREE

As Riley boarded her flight to Palm Beach, Rushi and Akshay cleared customs in Havana. As they walked through the doors of the un-air-conditioned terminal, humidity overwhelmed them. Even in winter, the humidity in Havana was stifling compared to the high desert at home.

Havana hadn't changed much since 1958, when Castro rolled into town. Vintage cars, dating from the 1950s, still served as taxis, threading down the pot-holed streets. The boulevards were lined with an eclectic mix of old and new architecture, reflecting the fifty years of economic isolation Cuba endured, followed by an intermittent influx of European and Middle Eastern capital.

The Russians always had an interest in Cuba. At first, it was a leverage point during the Cold War, then the Russian mob used it as a way to smuggle people and products into and out of the U.S. Corruption in Cuban government was accepted as normal business, so the Russians operated unchallenged.

Al-Qaeda was quick to ally itself with Cuba, realizing that for money, they could get whatever they wanted with no questions asked. While the new American administration was having its *Kumbaya* moment and trying to convince the American people, *If we don't bother them, they won't bother us,* Al-Qaeda established a base of operations just ninety miles from the US coastline.

Rushi walked to the taxi stand and handed a piece of paper with the bank address on it to the dispatcher, who promptly turned and signaled the next cab in line, a 1958 Marathon, to pull up. The four-wheeled behemoth, featured suicide doors and no air-conditioning.

The dispatcher leaned into the window to speak with the driver, then returned to the curb. "Twenty dollars."

Akshay nodded. The official currency of Cuba was the peso, but it held no value outside the country, creating a huge black market for foreign currency. Dollars were king, followed by the Euro.

"You pay now, please." The dispatcher extended his hand, opening and closing his fingers quickly.

Akshay dug into his pocket and produced twenty Euros. The dispatcher grabbed it and opened the door.

As the boys climbed in, he said, "Sorry, no change," and closed the door. Before either could reply, the cab pulled away from the curb, swerving into traffic.

"We just got screwed," Akshay said.

"No shit, Goat Boy. Welcome to Cuba."

"What do you mean, Goat Boy?"

"If that goat on the train could get over on you, then the taxi dispatcher probably saw you coming a mile away."

"Oh? Now I get advice from Mr. World Traveler? It's me, Rushi. I've know you since you were born. You've never been more than fifty miles from home. Spare me the lecture on street smarts and focus on the job. If we screw this up, we're as good as dead."

"Great. Now you're Mr. Dramatic."

The taxi sped around a corner, throwing the boys against the door.

"Hey, we might die right here in this cab."

Tires squealed.

"How much farther?" Akshay asked the driver in English.

"No hablo Ingles."

Neither boy had shaved or showered in over forty-eight hours. Not only were they terrorists, but they looked the part.

The cab screeched to a halt in front of the Credit Suisse bank office.

"Aqui." The driver pointed at the bank.

The boys slid to the curb side of the car, dragging their bags behind them. The moment the door closed, the cab pulled away.

Within five steps inside the bank, two uniformed security guards approached. "Do you need help?" one asked.

"We need to see Mr. Mubarak."

"Mubarak." The guard parroted as he eyeballed the two youths, who looked very out of place.

"Wait here," the other guard said.

A few minutes later, a tall, dark-skinned man in his late fifties, wearing a meticulously tailored suit and Bruno Magli wingtips, walked down the stairs and stopped to speak with a guard. Glancing at the two boys from across the lobby, he nodded and dismissed the guard.

Rushi couldn't take his eyes off the man's huge gold watch that probably cost as much as a house.

"I am Mubarak," the man said. "What can I do for you?" He shamelessly spoke loud enough to be overheard by the guard.

Rushi pulled the lanyard with the key from around his neck and handed it to the man.

"I see. And your name is?"

"Rushi Kumar Ali."

"Very well. Please follow me." Forcing a thin smile, he tried to ignore the stench from the two travelers.

The boys followed the banker to a small room off the lobby in direct sight of the massive safe door.

"Wait here, please," Mubarak said.

A minute later, he reentered the room with a large safety-deposit box. He positioned himself so the ceiling-mounted camera wouldn't record a direct image of his face when he spoke.

"I'll leave this here with you. Please take your time. I'll close the door. Ring this bell when you're done, and I'll return to put away the box for you."

He left the room, closing the door behind him. The boys sat down and lifted the lid from the box.

It was another day at the Turban. Phillipa Barnes, Bob's manager, arrived exactly on time to unlock the door. Phil was an ex-cop and 911 dispatcher. Her husband ditched her like an AIDS patient when she was diagnosed with Multiple Sclerosis, leaving her with two kids and a mortgage. Bob and Phil went to the academy together, and, when he opened the bar, she needed a job. She looked butch and was able to drink like a man, but she abstained since her diagnosis. She smoked like a cannon and cursed like a Marine on shore leave.

She did a great job with the clientele, speaking fluent redneck and cop. Grateful to Bob for the job, she was completely loyal. Bob never had to count the cash drawer when Phil was in charge.

All cops have nicknames or handles bestowed on them by other cops. Phillipa was nicknamed "Pancho," after Pancho Barnes, the famous aviatrix and owner of Pancho's Happy Bottom Riding Club, a bar and some said whorehouse that graced the famous Edwards Air Force Base. Back in the 1940s and '50s, that was where legends were made.

Sliding open the gate, Phil pondered how her body would endure shoveling the snow that quickly piled on the sidewalk. By six o'clock, the bar would be packed with cops, firemen, and EMTs, plus an eclectic group of city workers and hospital employees. The bar was a blue-collar, right-wing, "give-me-back-my-country" shrine. Bob was shocked when he saw the first batch of *You can find me at the Dirty Turban* T-shirts sold out in one week. Two years later, they still sold hats, bumper stickers, and jackets as fast as Bob could order them. In the summer months, a steady flow of tourists streamed through town just to have a drink at The Turban.

Occasionally, a right-wing radio talk-show host had Bob on

the show, but the single most-important event in the popularization of the bar was a live show Rush Limbaugh hosted on the Fourth of July. Since then, The Turban stood as a daily reminder of all that was wrong with American politics.

Bob couldn't have been happier. It might have cost him his job, but it gave him a cause, and he showed up every night to play to the converted. It wasn't for his ego or a need to be recognized. It was just his way of remaining a thorn in the side of the establishment that ruined him and his perfect career record. That, he suspected, was why The Turban was so popular with the law-enforcement community.

To Bob, it was all show. He arrived around six to hang out with the guys, shoot pool, throw darts, or watch a ball game or news on TV. By eight, he went home. When Riley was away, though, there was no rush to leave, so he stayed till closing.

Tonight he was scheduled to make the opening comments at the local Police Benevolence Association dinner. The Turban had a private room in the back that became the location of choice for off-site management meetings for all the local police departments. The walls were plastered with photos and news clippings of cops and soldiers killed in the line of duty and letters of support, encouragement, and thanks from people all across the country. Ordinary people were glad to know there were still men like Bob willing to stand up and be noticed.

It wasn't a shrine to Bob but to the ideals with which he was associated. At first, he felt uneasy about all the attention. It was never about him and never would be. After a while, he realized it was

OK to be thanked for doing public service.

Riley had the idea of putting the clippings on the walls, and, like all of her ideas, it was a popular addition. The room was booked five nights a week. It would be a busy night, and Pancho knew it.

The bar door flew open, breaking her train of thought. Carlos had arrived with the day's delivery.

"Where do you want it?" he asked from behind a stack of boxes.

"In the kitchen." She motioned toward the kitchen doors. Carlos and Ramon were a father-and-son delivery crew who worked for the local restaurant-supply house. They delivered to The Turban since it opened, and every day, they asked the same question, only to be directed to the kitchen.

Between then and four o'clock in the afternoon, food, beverages, and anything else needing delivery arrived and was put away, only to be pulled out, prepared, and served a few hours later. The phone rang and the jukebox played in a continuous, choreographed dance that ended with the first patrons arrived at five-thirty.

Bob woke to the pawing of Chance, Riley's dog, a ten-year-old, half-Irish-Setter, half Retriever. Riley found him abandoned on a beach in Bonaire, and he was her constant sailing companion ever since. Chance took to life onboard a boat better than on land. Adept in the water, he probably sailed over 30,000 miles in his lifetime. Age and arthritis made Riley worry that if Chance went overboard, he might drown, and she couldn't live with that possibility. As much as she wanted him along, the stress of watching him every moment forced her to leave him home. It was the first time since he was a puppy they weren't together. Bob and Chance got along well, but the dog knew Riley went to sea without him.

"OK, Buddy. I'll take you out. In fact, I'll do one better and take you to work with me tonight. Sound like fun?"

Chance visited The Turban many times and was well-liked by the crew. They fed him better than any dog should be fed, and he liked the people and the noise.

Chance gave Bob the look dogs gave to their owners. Bob dragged himself off the couch and walked toward the door.

"Come on, Dog."

Chance followed obediently.

* * *

Akshay and Rushi had never been on a boat before. They had never seen an ocean, much less crossed one. The two quickly heaved their dinners over the side of the *Scarab*, a go-fast boat that was the preferred choice for high-end human traffickers. They knew the Department of Defense shut down the heliostats at Boca Chica Naval Air Station as a cost-cutting measure. The new administration, looking for money to fund its appetite for social programs, didn't think twice about cutting the defense budget.

Their penchant for transparency, as they called it, led them to post the cuts on the Internet for anyone to see, including America's enemies.

No one watched, as the boys roared across the Florida Straits in excess of sixty miles an hour. They'd arrive in Miami in less than an hour. Another brother of the *jihad* would wait to meet them and drive them to Palm Beach. As sick as they were, they were awed by how easy it was to move from halfway around the world without being noticed or detected.

The sound of the twin-turbocharged Detroit Diesel 892s bellowing through open headers was deafening. The pounding of the sea against the hull was relentless and brutal, while the humidity was higher than they ever imagined. After sleeping on the train and plane, eating little, and indulging before boarding the boat, they were near exhaustion and too weak to speak, not that it mattered. Neither could hear anything over the engines and the wind.

Miami's lights twinkled in the distance. Getting into America was easy. A three-quarter moon rose over the eastern horizon. A few boats were out fishing, their lights blazing in the darkness, while the *Scarab's* lights were dark.

Rushi clutched the seat back in front of him, trying to figure out how they would survive their mission. His first experience with boats was miserable, but the first leg of the journey was a little over 100 miles. Their next ocean voyage would be nearly three times that distance, and they'd be piloting the boat in just over twenty-four hours. For the moment, surviving the passage consumed all his thoughts. Whenever he felt he might fail, he concentrated on avenging his father. Vengeance gave him the motivation to press on and the incentive to risk both their lives. If they were caught, the worst that could happen would be they'd be sent home, meaning a death sentence for themselves and their families.

That led to the other motivational factor—fear of failure. He saw the consequences of failure when families he knew his entire life were slaughtered in public when someone failed the *jihad.*

Failure wasn't an option. Their mission was simple, and she was just a woman, while they were men. They would not fail.

Bob and Chance walked through the door of The Turban at five minutes before seven. As expected, the place was packed. The noise and bustle took Bob's mind off Riley.

"Hey, Boss."

"Evening, Pancho. How's every little thing?" He pulled off his coat and hung it on the back of his special chair. The only thing Bob reserved for himself was the first barstool in the corner. No one ever sat there but him.

Chance headed toward the kitchen, knowing where he would find food.

"Peachy," Pancho said, "You need to address the PBA dinner in the back room in about...." she paused dramatically to look at her watch, "thirty seconds, right?"

Her comment was metaphorical and sarcastic. She loved to tease him about his effortless ability to be on time within one minute for everything.

"Yeah, I got that."

"You want dinner?"

"Sounds good. What are the specials?"

"We got in twelve salmon steaks today. Want me to hold one for you?"

"That's a good action plan. I'll be done back there by eight, so have them put it up around a quarter to."

"Done. Riley get off OK?"

"Nary a hitch." His expression showed that her departure was a sensitive subject. "If I'm not out of there by eight, send in someone and say there's a phone call for me. Otherwise, I might be stuck there all night."

"No problem, Boss."

Bob walked toward the back room to address the local PBA chapter. He was their claim to fame in the world of law enforcement, and they loved hearing him speak.

Irritated, Riley paced the dock like a caged animal. The provisioning truck was late. It was dark, she was tired, and rain began falling. Frustrated that the office was closed, she was ready to leave yet another scathing voicemail on their answering machine when she saw truck headlights coming toward the marina.

"About friggin' time," she mumbled, walking toward the truck. "Over here!" she called, waving to the driver, so he would park closer to the boat rather thank drag boxes of supplies across the dock.

The truck changed direction and came toward her.

"Where have you guys been?" she demanded. "You were supposed to be here by six. It's almost eight."

"Sorry," the driver said from inside the darkened cabin. "We're running late."

"Well, let's get on with it. Grab my stuff and follow me."

Akshay and Rushi climbed down from the cab and went to

the rear of the truck, raising the roll-up door. It was a good thing Riley hadn't walked to the back of the truck with them. The boxes shifted in traffic, and the bodies of the driver and his assistant were in plain sight.

Each boy lifted two cartons of food and followed Riley. She was halfway back to the boat, stuffing her cell phone into her pocket, as she walked. She boarded, glanced back to see where her supplies were, and went to the main salon. The boys were a few steps behind her.

"Put down those boxes and get the rest while I start putting things away."

The two walked down the steps into the cabin, set down the boxes, and looked at each other.

"Well, go on. Bring the rest of the stuff up here, so I can stow it." Riley placed her hands on her hips, annoyed that the two young men were so inept.

Hesitating, they looked at each other. It was time. Riley knew something wasn't right, but it was too late.

Akshay grabbed at her, but she was married to a cop for her entire adult life and grabbed his collar, swinging him around and shoving him against the refrigerator door, where the handle speared his back. She planted her knee in his crotch, and he doubled over in pain.

Riley turned to Rushi, who wasn't prepared for resistance of such magnitude. She landed a right cross on his cheek that sent him to the floor, but, as she bolted for the door, she tripped over one of the boxes they delivered and dumped the contents across the floor.

Akshay grabbed her from behind and covered her mouth and nose with a rag soaked in chloroform. Dichloromethane wasn't very high tech, but it was cheap, effective, and easy to find.

Riley planted an elbow in his ribs, but Akshay hung on. She could handle the boys OK, but she was no match for chloroform. The last thing she remembered was her face hitting the floor and Akshay collapsing on top of her.

"Shit!" He rolled off her motionless body and lay panting on the floor. "I think she broke a rib."

"I don't want to hear it." Rushi's eye was already swollen shut from Riley's punch. "We need to get going. You park the truck and get the boat. Pull up beside this one while I wrap her up."

Akshay lifted himself off the floor, wincing in pain, as he crawled up the steps, looked around, and stuck his head through the hatch, at the dark and quiet marina.

Rushi took a roll of plastic stretch wrap from one of the boxes and wrapped Riley. She wouldn't have another chance to swing at him.

In what seemed like an hour but was only a few minutes, he heard the sound of an outboard motor arrive outside.

A moment later, Akshay pushed his head through the hatch. "Ready?"

"Yeah. Come down here and help me drag her on deck."

A few minutes later, they had Riley on the floor of a plain, white, center-console fishing boat.

"The marina's just a few minutes from the inlet," Rushi said. "We'll be in the open sea in no time, and then we're home free." He pulled a handheld GPS from his pocket.

"Home-free my ass. We have nearly 300 miles of open-ocean to cross, most of it in the dark." Akshay winced in pain.

"Get your shit together. She's a girl. Do you want them to think you can't handle a girl? Go sit up front. I'll get us past the inlet. If we see another boat, pretend we're going fishing or something."

"Great plan. I'm spitting blood, and you're worried that they'll think...."

"Sit down, or I'll kill you myself!"

The look in Rushi's eyes frightened Akshay, who was in no condition to confront his cousin. Obediently, he sat.

Rushi released the line holding them to the dock and pushed off, advancing the throttle on the outboard motor. Rushi was too tired to be scared, too scared to fail, and too full of vengeance to care what Akshay said. They had their prize. Their mission was to deliver her to an island in the Bahamas, the coordinates to which were programmed into his GPS.

It was dark, but the moon was rising, the weather clear, the wind light, and the seas not nearly as rough as the previous night. They didn't need to move quickly, they just needed to be moving.

As they passed through the inlet into the open sea, they heard waves crashing against the breakwater. Once outside, all they had to do was point the boat where the GPS indicated and not stop. It would take at least ten hours before they reached their destination, and then their obligation would be fulfilled.

He could do that. He had to.

The Dirty Turban

CHAPTER FOUR

Bob was most of the way through his salmon dinner. He took refuge from the ruckus in the Turban in what passed for his office, so he could eat in peace. The bar was still packed, and Chance was curled up under the desk, sleeping off his meal. The office had once been a closet, but Bob needed a place where he could actually run his business, so he converted the tiny ten by twelve foot walk-in.

The door had one-way glass, so he could see out, but no one could see in. A small, flat-screen TV hung on the wall over his desk. A computer occupied most of the desk, but he pushed stacks of bills aside to make room for his dinner.

It was an uneventful day. Bob sat with his feet on the corner of the desk, enjoying a cup of Irish coffee and watching the news when he heard a knock at the door.

"Come in." He pulled his feet off the desk, because he never let an employee see him with his feet up, a habit left over from his law-enforcement days.

"Hey, Boss," Pancho said. "There's a call for you on line two."

"Aren't you a little late with that? I told you to do that only if I was stuck in that PBA thing."

"No, there really is a call for you on line two." She chuckled.

"Oh. Who is it?"

"I don't know. She said her name was Carol, I think."

"Don't look at me like that, Panch. She and her husband are Riley's crew."

"I wasn't looking for an explanation." With a Cheshire-cat grin, she closed the door before he could reply.

Bob swiveled his chair around and lifted the receiver from its cradle, punching the line button in one motion. "Hey, Carol. How are things?"

"Bob, I don't really know."

"What's that supposed to mean?" He leaned forward in his chair, rested his elbows on the desk while rubbing his eyes with his free hand.

"Have you heard from Riley lately?"

He stopped his random thoughts and focused on the voice. "Not in the last eight hours. Why?"

"Ritchie and I got to the boat, but she isn't here, and there were a couple boxes of unstowed supplies sitting on the deck. I called her cell, but there's no answer. If she went out to get something, she didn't leave a note or anything, and the stuff on the deck is all over the place. I didn't have your cell number, but I called information for the bar number, and...."

"No, no, no. You did the right thing to call me. I haven't spoken with her since lunchtime, but she told me she would be waiting for the provisioner to deliver food. Maybe they forgot something, and she ran out to get it. I know she wanted to sail at first light. Let me try her phone, and we'll give her another hour. Then I'll call you back. What's a good number for you?"

"The satellite phone's sitting right here. Just call that one. I'll leave it on."

"OK. That'll work. I'll call you back."

"All right, Bob. If she shows up first, I'll call you."

"Good. 'Bye." He hung up and sat still, his mind racing. Picking up his Blackberry, he dialed Riley. She might ignore a call from Carol, but she always took his calls.

An overwhelming sense of uneasiness washed over him. Riley was probably the most-reachable woman on earth. She answered the phone even if she was in the shower.

Turning on his computer, he waited for it to finish booting. He could track Riley on the computer via her cell phone's GPS. The boot cycle seemed to take an hour.

Finally, typing one key at a time with one finger, he typed the URL for the tracking site, logged in, and entered Riley's phone number. Her cell phone was eleven miles east of Palm Beach.

"That's impossible," he said. "That's the middle of the friggin' ocean!"

Incredulous, he thought the GPS must be wrong. Maybe she lost her phone. There was no logical explanation for such a location, because the boat was still at the dock.

He sat for a moment, staring at the screen, trying to come up with a plausible explanation for what he saw, when suddenly, the target disappeared from the map.

"What the...?" He looked at his watch. It was almost eleven o'clock. Something wasn't right.

* * *

Halfway around the world, KSM and his entourage stepped out of a pair of black limousines. The bodyguards went first, then the tall one, and finally KSM emerged from the vehicles into brilliant sunlight on the ramp at Kuwait City International Airport.

There to greet him was his third cousin, Malich al Sabah, a direct descendent of the Kuwaiti royal family and an outspoken supporter of Al-Qaeda.

"Salaam Aleikum."

"Aleikum Salaam."

The two embraced and exchanged greetings. KSM was born in Kuwait but spent most of his time in Afghanistan.

"Good to see you, Cousin," KSM said.

"I'm glad to see you as well. There are many who are pleased to see that you have reenergized the *jihad* against the West. I made all the arrangements you requested. There will be no questions when you land. The reporters you selected are already onboard. They know they're going somewhere but nothing else."

"Excellent. You have my deepest gratitude. What we're about to do will change everything. We'll take our cause to the next level and will beat them with their own technology."

"Go with Allah, Cousin."

Al-Sabah stepped aside, waving the group toward the steps of his personal Global Express and hoping his cousin wouldn't introduce him to the tall one. The Global Express was the ride of choice for moving quickly around the world. Every rap artist, rock star, and Arab prince had one. It was *the* ultimate status symbol.

It would fly nonstop from Kuwait City to Georgetown on Great Exuma in the Bahamas. It did so once a month for almost a year, since Al-Sabah bought Musha Cay, an exclusive private island resort thirty-five miles north of Georgetown in the Exuma chain. Musha Cay (pronounced *key*) was developed by millionaire real-estate developer John Melk in the late 1990s. He sold it at the height of the real-estate boom to David Copperfield, the world-renowned entertainer and magician.

Then Musha Cay performed a magic trick even Copperfield couldn't comprehend. It made fifty-five million dollars disappear in two years of operation. It was a super-exclusive resort, like Peters Island or Bitter End in the British Virgin Islands, and it rented by the week for $350,000. The island housed only seventeen guest beds, and nearly as many staff lived and worked there full-time.

When Melk sold the island, it was booked twenty-two weeks a year, grossing more than eight million dollars annually and barely making a profit. The slumping economy and the need to use private air transport to reach the place, coupled with Copperfield's inept management team, turned it into a loss leader. When Al-Sabah went there to vacation and casually mentioned he might like to buy it, Copperfield saw his exit strategy, as Al-Sabah knew he would. It was the perfect forward base, disguised as a running business.

Musha Cay was very important to the local Bahaman economy, which was devastated by the slumping global economy.

The locals were thrilled to have Al-Sabah take over the island. When his jet arrived at Georgetown, a smaller Dehavilland Twin Otter, which came with the sale of the property, flew over from the tiny, crushed-coral runway on Rudder Cut Cay to take people and cargo to the island.

Musha Cay and Rudder Cut Cay had once been attached, but a hurricane cut them in two, leaving what passed for a runway 300 yards across open water from the dock at Musha Cay. Everyone and everything that flew into Rudder Cut had to cross those 300 yards of open water on two small boats working as island taxis. Once a month, a shallow-water fuel tanker delivered diesel fuel for the island's generators. Heavy construction equipment and material were shipped from Georgetown or Nassau on an LST vessel with a ramp in the bow.

Everyone knew the US military tracked all flights leaving Kuwait City, so Al-Sabah sent the flight every month at nearly the same time, whether he was onboard or not, to establish a pattern. Ironically, the new oil rich of the Middle East took to vacationing there and the island turned a profit simply because Al-Sabah owned it. Even Hugo Chavez of Venezuela frequented the island. He liked it so much he lobbied for and won the right to hold an OPEC meeting on the island.

Though Al-Sabah managed to increase the popularity and profitability of the island, that wasn't why he bought it. He was one of the new generation of Al-Qaeda. He stole a page from the Italian Mafia playbook and used legitimate businesses to mask the work of the illegitimate ones. He studied the business dealings of the

Colombian and Mexican drug cartels, who, twenty years earlier, established the profitability of illegal drug routes through the Caribbean. He researched how the Iranians, in the 1970s, under the Shah, used their diplomatic immunity to smuggle drugs into the US with the full knowledge of the State Department.

Musha Cay, close to the U.S., was an excellent traffic point to smuggle Afghan-grown heroin into the country. Heroin had always been Afghanistan's single-largest cash crop, and, other than terrorism, its number one export. The purchase of the island evolved into a cash pipeline that rivaled the Cali drug cartel. That it made a legitimate profit was a bonus.

The tall one advanced toward the air stair door. His name, rarely spoken, was Ali Hadan. Born in Yemen, he held a bachelor's degree from Boston College in journalism and a master's degree in political science. Living in the U.S. for almost ten years taught him perfect English, though he rarely spoke. If he hadn't been so tall, he might have been nicknamed the silent one.

He met KSM in Guantanamo. When the new U.S. administration released Hadan, he accompanied KSM to Afghanistan, quickly becoming his right-hand man and the number-three man in Al-Qaeda. His experience in the States allowed him to see things through Western eyes, a gift not lost on UBL, who was now dead. If Al-Qaeda was to survive and the *jihad* to continue, it needed the fresh insights of men like Hadan and the support of others like his cousin, motivated by the same Western greed they denounced.

The tall one and KSM had plenty of time to think about how to put a new face on the old *jihad*. Together, they created a plan to make a media event out of another attack on the U.S. They would use *Al Jazeera* to cover it like a sporting event, but from their point of view. It would show the Western nations that they could and would operate with impunity and in the open on satellite TV, not from a remote mountain cave. The plan would make the fight personal to the American people.

They would abduct a U.S. citizen from American soil, take the person to a foreign country, and threaten to behead him on live TV. That was KSM's contribution to the plan. He was responsible for the beheading of *Wall Street Journal* reporter Daniel Pearl and said so during his trial at Guantanamo. He was very proud of that act. The response from Western populations to such an atrocity was shock and fear.

Since Pearl was a reporter in a war zone and a Jew, too, his beheading was seen as positive among the extremists. Hadan convinced KSM that abducting a targeted U.S. citizen from American soil and the subsequent execution would frighten the American people and bring terror to a new level in the States. No one would feel safe. Beheading a woman would have no repercussions from the Islamic world, because Muslims considered women to be property.

To the West, killing a woman would be more effective in striking fear into the population than killing a man. KSM added to the drama by bringing a handpicked reporter and camera crew to film the event live. He would also hold out hope for the victim's life if certain conditions were met, forcing those who cared for her to choose between their country, values, faith, and family.

Once released from Gitmo, the two men learned of the failed

bombing attempt by Rushi's and Akshay's fathers and how Captain Hershey was treated by his own government. They chose Hershey's wife as their target, reasoning he might be willing to commit treason against his country to save her life. They never intended to let her live. Whether or not Hershey did what was asked, she would be executed on live TV, and there would be nothing the U.S. government or anyone else could do about it.

It was prime-time techno terrorism. It would be great theater, visual and graphic as well as humiliating and terrifying to the West. It would also play well at home, because most of the followers of radical Islamic sects were illiterate. TV and radio worked better for them than printed material.

That was the plan that Hadan explained to the two reporters from *Al Jazeera* sitting in the back of the Global Express.

"You two will be a witness to history," Hadan finished.

"We'll be witnessing a murder. I don't know if we can be part of this."

Mohesh Salawi, a young cameraman for *Al Jazeera,* covered combat in Iraq and Afghanistan and was sent to Mumbai in 2008 to cover the bombings in that city. His on-camera partner was Padma Rajput, an Indian woman, a rising star with the network. Rajput found a place at *Al Jazeera* accidentally, but the two were handpicked for this job for a reason. Both were young, career-minded, and wouldn't question authority, morality, or the legitimacy of what they saw.

Rajput reached across her seat and smacked her cameraman, adding a stare that said, *Shut up!*

"We're on a mission from Allah," Hadan said softly. "If it's so that someone must die, then it is so. I don't see doing God's work as a crime." He spoke slowly, as if to an innocent child.

"You may not see it as a crime, but in the eyes of a world court...."

"Enough!" Hadan interrupted Salawi in midsentence. The fury in his eyes and anger in his voice sent a rush of adrenalin through the young cameraman.

"Don't worry," Rajput said quickly. "We'll do exactly as you ask. If you want me to say something specific, let me know before the cameras roll, and we'll work it in."

"I count on you to carry our message clearly." Hadan's expression indicated he was working hard to remain calm. "I'll review our talking points with you before you go on the air."

Hadan glared at them before turning abruptly and walking to the front of the plane. The two reporters sat there, stunned. They were part of something far beyond the scope of normal journalism, if anyone could classify what *Al Jazeera* did as journalism.

"We could be executed for doing this!" Salawi whispered.

"We'll be executed if we don't!" she hissed back. "Get hold of yourself before you get us both killed."

They were smart enough to know their lives were in danger. They'd been in dangerous situations before, but they were able to identify the enemy. Suddenly, they weren't certain. As unhappy as they were to be part of such a grotesque publicity stunt, Al-Sabah was eager to be included. He installed a satellite uplink on Musha and developed a cover story to explain it, saying the island was rented by a Saudi-based conglomerate for an executive retreat. The fact that he wouldn't be on the plane gave him the plausible deniability he needed if anything went wrong. If the situation proceeded as planned, he had the cover of a legitimate business transaction.

The sun cleared the horizon a few minutes after six-thirty. Rushi stayed awake all night to keep their tiny craft on course. As the sky lightened, he saw his cousin curled in a ball on the bow pad, seeking shelter from the ocean spray behind a tiny canvas canopy. Riley lay motionless on deck.

As the sun broke through the clouds, the light blinded the exhausted helmsman. He was proud that he negotiated their way past Isaacs Light, a lighthouse on the uninhabited spit of land north of Bimini, on the westernmost outcropping of a shoal that claimed its fair share of mariners.

They were en route for eight hours, and, according to the GPS, they covered 176 miles of their 300-mile journey. Rushi reduced power on the outboard to idle, and the boat came down off the step, settling into a nearly calm sea. The wind was light all night, and they hadn't seen any other boats.

Unknown to them, the US Coast Guard saw them via a remote infrared camera on Isaacs.

As the boat idled, Rushi picked up the first of six plastic gas cans, pried open the cap, and inserted the tip of the nozzle into the fuel tank. Sitting on the gunnels while fuel transferred, he marveled at the beautiful scene. He never saw sunrise over an ocean before. He'd been running on pure adrenaline for eight hours and felt almost euphoric as the last of the drug faded.

The first can empty, he turned to the next. Akshay awakened as if from a bad dream, sat up, holding his ribcage and wincing in pain.

"What time is it, Cousin?" Akshay grunted.

"Almost a quarter to seven in the morning. You slept all night."

"Where are we?"

"Between Nassau and Andros. Right where we're supposed to be."

"How much longer?"

"If the GPS is right, about 125 more miles, maybe six hours."

Akshay stood and moved to the back of the boat. He slowly stretched his damaged rib from side-to-side. "I've got to piss." He stepped onto the small swim platform at the stern.

"Don't fall in. You can't swim."

"I'm more concerned about a shark trying to bite off my dick."

"I wouldn't worry about that too much. Your dick's hardly worth the effort."

"Shit! That bitch kicked me so hard, I'm pissing blood." He zipped up his fly and scrambled back into the boat, sitting on the gunnel to catch his breath.

"Don't worry. You won't die from it."

"Gee, thanks for the sympathy. I'm pissing blood, and you make jokes." His tan complexion was ashen gray. He felt nauseated by the sight of his own blood, but there was nothing he could do about it.

"You're the one who let a girl kick your ass. If I were you, I wouldn't mention that to anyone. Get off your ass and help me finish transferring gas into the tank."

Together, they emptied the cans into the main tank.

"I don't suppose you remembered to bring anything to eat," Rushi said.

"I took fruit and veggies from the truck when I parked it. There's a six-pack of bottled water behind that seat cooler." He pointed at the bow seat beside where Riley lay.

Akshay flipped open the lid and took out two bottles of water and two apples, tossing one of each to his cousin.

Riley woke. She couldn't get her eyes to focus in the developing daylight. She was overcome by a wave of nausea from an overdose of chloroform. Coughing, she found her mouth taped shut.

Akshay saw her struggled to breathe but continued eating his apple. Riley squirmed in the stretch wrap but couldn't move.

"Take the tape off her mouth," Rushi said.

"No. Let her suffer."

"If she dies, we die."

Akshay, considering that for a moment, realized Rushi was right, though he wanted to extract as much retribution on Riley as he could. He reached down and violently ripped the tape from her mouth.

Riley gasped for breath and coughed. Unable to fight the bile rising in her throat, she vomited on the deck. Panting where she lay, she tried to fight off the drugs after effects. "Water." She sqeaked.

"Give her water, Akshay."

Displeased by the idea of doing anything for the woman, Akshay tipped the water bottle in his hand and poured it in a stream three feet above her head.

Riley turned her head and opened her mouth to catch some, then swallowed. Catching her breath, she managed, "Thank you."

"You won't thank me for long."

Still confused, trying to remember what happened, she asked, "Who are you? What do you want from me?"

"Enough questions. You made me piss blood!" He leaned over to replace the tape on her mouth.

"Wait! Please, I can't breathe. Please don't tape my mouth." She shook her head, fear showing in her eyes.

After savoring her fear, Akshay said, "OK, but if you make a sound, I'll kill you right here."

He brought his face closer to hers for dramatic value. Riley wasn't stupid and knew that if they wanted her dead, she'd already *be* dead. She didn't know who they were, but she could make a pretty good guess. She and Bob surmised there was the possibility of retribution for what Bob did. They thought it would be targeted at him, though she was a possible target, too. Since no better explanation came to mind, that was her conclusion. Assessing her options, she decided to play helpless blonde and see where it led.

"I promise not to give you any trouble. Is there any chance you can let me sit up for a while? I can't feel my arms, and...."

"Shut up!" Akshay snapped.

"Sit her up, Akshay," Rushi said.

Akshay glared at his cousin. Rushi stepped out from behind the center console and pulled Riley upright with her back to the bow. She leaned against the bulkhead, sitting on the deck.

"Don't make me sorry I did that for you," he warned, "or I'll let my cousin do what he wants with you."

It was an idle threat, though it sounded credible. Riley nodded and kept an expression of *Why are you doing this to me?* in her eyes as she looked at him.

"Are you capable of steering a straight course, Cousin?" Rushi asked.

"Yes. Why?"

"Because while you slept, I couldn't, and I'm exhausted. If you can keep us on course, I'd like to close my eyes for an hour or two, if that's OK with you." Sarcasm dripped from his words.

"I'm sure I can do it."

"Three thousand RPM on the tachometer will give you about twenty knots. Any faster, and the boat pounds too hard. Twenty knots keeps us on schedule."

"I can do it."

"Wake me if there's a problem. Time for one more thing before we start again."

He pulled the SAT phone from the backpack he had clipped to a leaning post. Once it powered up, he pushed speed dial and 01. The phone dialed itself.

51,000 feet over the eastern Atlantic, the phone on the bulkhead beside Hadan's head rang. He answered on the first ring.

"Yes."

"It's Rushi."

"Go on."

"We have your package, and we're on time."

"How long before you arrive?"

"About six hours."

"Any problems?"

"None."

"Good. We'll be waiting for you."

"I understand."

Hadan, pushing the *End Call* button, felt annoyed, because Rushi used his own name on the phone, but at least he hadn't used Hadan's name. The U.S. monitored all kinds of electronic communications around the globe, and the wrong word would flag the call. Fortunately, they'd be on the ground in three hours.

Rushi pushed the *End-Call* button, turned off the power to the phone, and replaced it in his backpack.

"All right. See the GPS?" he asked Akshay, pointing to the GPS mounted in a bracket on the windscreen. "You stay on 130 degrees on the compass. Just keep the little black boat on the little pink line on the screen, and it'll take us where we need to go."

"Got it. 130 degrees."

"There's nothing between here and there. The next land you see is where we're going. There's nothing to hit, just a straight line through the water."

Riley overheard them. She didn't know where she was but in

six hours, they would be a couple of hundred miles southeast. There was little she could do but sit quietly and wait for an opportunity.

Rushi climbed over Riley and onto the bow to crawl under the canopy. "You behave," he told the back of Riley's head, as he laid his head on the dock fender that pushed up against the gunnels.

Akshay advanced the throttle to 3,000 RPM. The little boat accelerated, as he adjusted the throttle to maintain that speed. The hull beat rhythmically against the sea. He soon had a feel for the helm and had no trouble staying on course.

Within two minutes, the exhausted Rushi passed into REM sleep. Riley struggled to find a comfortable position that wouldn't beat her body against the unpadded Fiberglas of the deck.

They had six hours to go.

* * *

"Keep it on the centerline. Good. Now taxi over the hold short line and stop the aircraft, then go to your after-landing checklist."

It was another day in paradise for Keith Michaels, speaking into the boom mic of his headset. He cracked open the door with his knee to allow cool morning air into the stuffy cockpit. A pilot his entire life, he managed to make a career and a living doing what he loved.

"Good. Now, what did you miss?" He didn't wait for an answer. "Boost pumps off."

He had a dream career in aviation. After leaving the Air Force, he earned his flight instructor's certificates and mechanic's ratings. He even went to civilian test-pilot school in Mohave,

California, which earned him a production test-pilot job at Piper Aircraft Company in Vero Beach, Florida. When that grew old, he landed a coveted airline job with Trans World Airlines. That gig lasted four years and ended when the famed airline went bankrupt.

He started a jet charter company, flying people like Warren Buffett and Jimmy Buffet. His life became an episode of the *Lifestyles of the Rich and Famous.* He had more fun than any self-employed individual had a right to and thanked God the government couldn't tax or regulate fun.

Michaels sold his business at the height of the fractional-jet ownership boom and received top dollar for it. Thinking retirement would be easy, he discovered, much to his chagrin, that when his son left for college, all Michaels wanted to do with his free time was fly. For entertainment value, he returned to flight instruction, teaching airline pilots of tomorrow the lessons of the past.

Leaning against the doorframe as his student taxied the little twin-engine airplane, he took a deep breath of the cool morning air and reveled in how much he still loved flying. Even after 10,000 flight hours, it hadn't grown old.

He thought of Ernest Gann, his favorite author, who wrote *Fate Is the Hunter.* Gann was a famous pilot and author, but the book wasn't about flying. It was all about when to hold 'em and when to fold 'em. Michaels read it three times before figuring out what Gann meant. It certainly wasn't time for him to fold 'em.

As the little Beechcraft taxied past the main terminal building toward the hangar, he saw a familiar silhouette waiting on the tarmac and realized it was Bob.

"OK. Now go to your shutdown checklist," Michaels said automatically, wondering to what he owed the honor of an early-morning visit from his friend.

As the engines shuddered to a stop, Michaels removed his headset, noting the time on his flight log, and climbed out of the plane.

"Hey, Man!" He greeted Bob with a smile, handshake, and a hug. "You didn't tell me you were coming down this soon. Guess you got tired of freezing your ass off, eh? How are things?"

Bob didn't answer, and he didn't smile.

"What's wrong, Dude?" Michaels lowered his voice, seeing the distress on his friend's face.

"Something's happened to Riley," Bob forced himself to say.

"What do you mean?"

"I got a call last night from her crew. She didn't show up at the boat. I called her phone and didn't get an answer, then I used the GPS tracker, and it showed her phone was somewhere offshore before I lost the signal. I called the GPS tracking company. They confirmed it wasn't a system error, so I went to the Atlantic City Airport and chartered a plane.

"I got here at four-thirty this morning. When I reached the boatyard, it was crawling with cops. They found a truck in the parking lot owned by the provisioner Riley uses. The driver and his helper were in the back, both dead. Riley's boat was a mess. They think it's an abduction." He spoke like the cop he was, cool, calm, and detached.

"What do you think?"

"I don't know what to think. There are no threats or ransom requests. I don't get it."

"What do you need?"

"If it's an abduction, they'll try to contact me, so I may need to get back to Jersey in a hurry."

"I've got that covered. I manage a Pilatus PC-12 for someone. It'll get us there in four hours. When was the last time you slept?"

"I got a few hours' sleep on the flight down."

"All right. How about you head over to my house, grab a shower, and get some clean clothes? Whatever you need, you got."

Bob didn't answer. Michaels couldn't tell if he was exhausted or in deep thought. Bob turned toward the car and walked off.

The Global Express touched down on the runway at Exuma International, better known as Georgetown. The original Georgetown Airport was five miles farther south, but it was in terrible shape and was rarely used. The Exuma International Airport was built as part of a deal between the government of the Bahamas and private investors to lure the Four Seasons hotel chain to build on the island. The airport was built, but it remained a Bahamian airport—no security, services, or worries.

As the engines spooled down, the air stair door dropped slowly to the ground. Beside the jet sat the Twin Otter, the island used to shuttle people and cargo back and forth. The runway at Rudder Cut Cay was only 2,000 feet long, far too short for any jet.

As his entourage deplaned, KSM sat motionless with his

sunglasses on, watching every person onboard walk past, which gave
Padma and Mohesh the creeps. They scurried past as quickly as they
could without bumping into the next person ahead. They walked
straight to the Otter, where two Bahamian handlers moved luggage
and equipment from one plane to the other.

The Otter's captain started the right engine, while the copilot
loaded passengers and cargo for the twelve-minute flight to Rudder
Cut Cay. Hadan walked to a uniformed Bahamian Customs Officer
and handed him a plain manila envelope.

"I believe everything you need is in here," he said.

"I'm sure it is, Sir." He smiled and extended his hand to
shake.

Hadan ignored him, turned, and walked to the running Otter.
KSM just walked up the boarding step, as the left engine began
turning. The copilot stood beside the door, waiting for Hadan. The
smell of jet fuel and the overwhelming humidity disgusted him,
reminding him of Cuba. He longed for the desert.

The whine of engines increased, as Hadan boarded the last
step. The copilot climbed in behind him to close the door, and the
aircraft lurched forward.

"Skip the passenger briefing and come up here," the captain
shouted to the young first officer.

That was an unusual request from a professional captain, but
the copilot complied. They flew in wordless silence at 1,000 feet
above some of the most-spectacular tropical islands on earth. Twelve
minutes later, the aircraft rolled out on final approach, pivoting
directly over the submerged fuselage of another aircraft that crashed

after a failed takeoff from Rudder Cut. The plane was still visible through the shallow, emerald-green water.

As the Otter lined up for what passed as a runway, Hadan frowned. The runway was nothing more than a crushed-coral road with water on both ends. It looked small to him, as he peered over his shoulder through the front windshield.

The plane was made for such a landing, and the pilot showed his skill by getting the aircraft down and stopping in less than half the usable length. Throwing the big turboprops into reverse and tapping the brakes, he brought the plane to a complete stop, pivoted, and taxied back to the end of the runway. The copilot climbed out of his seat and turned toward his passengers, who were already unbuckling their seat belts.

"OK, Everybody. If you'd please exit the aircraft through the same door you boarded...." He didn't know what to say. He was told a Saudi company rented the island for a retreat, and that was all he wanted to know.

He pulled the door latch release firmly, and a blast of hot air and dust blew in through the doorway. It was almost noon, and, though it was winter, it was hot.

A group of Musha employees waited for the plane. Part of their job was to load and unload the plane and help transport everything to the waiting boats, then to the island. The process took only a few minutes.

The most senior of the Musha crew was an aging white Bahamian whom everyone called Caretaker. He'd been on Musha since before Melk purchased the property. He hired and fired everyone but the property manager, to whom he reported.

That was how things were done in the Bahamas. To run a business, Bahamians must be hired. Caretaker had to be over seventy, but no one was sure. In the Bahamas, age was irrelevant. His leathery, permanently tanned skin reflected a lifetime of labor in the sun. But he was still strong and did his job.

All the Bahamians respected him, and he was one of the few individuals who could get things done in anything close to a reasonable timeframe. In the Bahamas, no one asked what time it was, because it was always Bahamas time.

In a few minutes, Caretaker orchestrated the movement of people and materials from the plane to the boats. The passengers went first, and the cargo would follow. It wouldn't do to have guests sitting in the hot sun while cargo was moved.

Most of the entourage boarded the boats, leaving two guards behind to keep the Bahamians honest. The boats sped across the 300 yards of open water in one minute, disgorging their passengers onto the dock at Musha.

Cindy Fink, Al-Sabah's handpicked property manager, waited for them. Tall and leggy, she was a late-thirties, auburn-haired Canadian. She drank the *Jihadist* Kool-Aid and was a sympathizer to the cause. Though she knew none of the details about what was happening or who her guests were, she knew it had to do with promoting the holy war upon the West. That was all she needed.

"Hello, Everyone, and welcome. I'm Cindy Fink, the property manager on the island and the person responsible for making sure your every wish comes true."

She meant it. In the three years she ran the island for Al-Sabah, she procured everything from hookers and illegal drugs to rare food and wine, all to please the patrons' whims. She even had twelve wild pheasants flown in, so one client could hunt them during his stay.

"If you would follow me to the Great House, we've prepared refreshments for you after your long flight. This allows us time to have your luggage moved from the airstrip. If you require anything special, let me know. We send the Otter to Georgetown once a day to pick up provisions, but we would be happy to send it anywhere to get what you desire. If you'd please follow me...."

She turned and walked toward the Great House.

The tall one turned to KSM. "If they're on time, we can make the evening news," KSM grunted.

"Don't be in a hurry, Ali. She's only been missing for a few hours. The longer we wait, the more places she could be—Cuba, South America, anywhere. Make them sweat."

The tall one turned to a guard. "When the gear arrives, send the TV equipment to the Great House right away and post the guards. Put a lookout at the top of the hill facing west, and let me know when you see them coming."

"As you wish." The guard jumped into the boat, as it pulled away from the dock.

CHAPTER FIVE

Bob fell asleep on the couch. Though he was exhausted, his cell phone woke him immediately.

"Hello?" he said into his beat-up Blackberry.

"Robert Hershey?"

"Yes."

"Captain Hershey, this is Special Agent Wagner from the FBI."

"I'm here."

"Captain, I'm following up as a courtesy to Deputy Miller's office. We have a request regarding the possible abduction of your wife."

"Go on."

Hershey knew Miller personally. He ran the Los Angeles Police Department's Special Crimes Division, and Hershey held a similar position with New Jersey State. They met at a conference years earlier and stayed in touch. Miller even testified as a character witness at Hershey's Congressional hearing.

"Captain, as I'm sure you're familiar with FBI protocols, we're currently interfacing with the Palm Beach County Sheriff's office, which is on the scene. Once we have the forensics report...."

"Hold on, Agent Wagner. Let me save you some time. I've been doing this kind of work since before you were born. I believe she's been taken out of the country against her will, and...."

Wagner cut him off. "Captain, I'm aware of your record. That's the reason for the courtesy call. I'm sure you appreciate the need to follow protocols and...."

Bob was not in the mood for bureaucratic bullshit. He needed men, equipment, and, more importantly, information. "Special Agent, can I speak with your supervisor, please?" He tried to control his rage.

"Captain, my supervisor isn't available right now, but if I can have a number where he can...."

Bob pressed the *End-Call* button, so he wouldn't say something he would regret.

Michaels walked into the room. "Who was that?"

"Oh, the Fee-Bees. They were making a courtesy call."

"A what?" His expression was quizzical.

"Never mind. Let's call Brian, then can we return to Jersey? I'll ask him to meet us at the bar. If there's going to be a ransom call, they'll call Jersey, not here."

"Sure. You want to pick him up on the way? It's only an hour and twenty minutes out of our way. Then you guys can talk on the plane. It's got a SAT phone, so if you want to work the phones, you can."

"That would be great." Bob sat silently, his mind in deep thought.

"Dude, we'll find her." Michaels placed his hand on his buddy's shoulder.

"I know," Bob said solemnly.

The Pilatus touched down at the Cuyahoga County Airport at exactly 7:00 PM Eastern Standard Time and taxied to the ramp. Michaels keyed the *Push-to-Talk* button on his boom mic.

"Cleveland Jet Center, Pilatus 769 Juliet Bravo."

"769 JB, go ahead," a cheerful female voice answered.

"Sixty-nine Jay Bee is a quick turn, top the tanks, with Prist, and oh—one more thing. I need a ground power unit during the turn. I want to keep the heaters running."

"No problem. The linemen will be waiting for you. By the way, there's a policeman in the lobby waiting for you."

"That's no policeman. That's Brian." He knew Brian would be within earshot of the radio.

"Just thought you should know."

Michaels smiled. He liked to play a little game with himself and wondered if the voice matched its owner. She sounded cute on the radio, so she was probably overweight, divorced, and bitter.

As the big Pratt and Whitney turboprop spun down, the linemen appeared with a ground power unit and plugged it into the plane. Michaels checked the ammeter, confirmed the hookup, and turned on the radiant heaters to keep the cabin warm. It was fourteen degrees in Cleveland, and Bob was asleep in the back seat of the massive cabin.

Michaels climbed out of his seat, glanced at Bob, who was snoring, and opened the cabin door before climbing down onto the frozen tarmac. The wind went right through him. One thing about flying corporately that he didn't miss was winter.

"Hey, Nukem," Brian said.

"Hey, Gunny." They shook hands and shoulder-bumped in one motion. "How's the county's youngest police chief doing?"

"Well, it's aging me." Brian flashed his infectious grin.

A fuel truck arrived.

"Top it with Prist?" the driver asked from the warm comfort of his cab.

"You got it!" Michaels said. Turning to Brian, he said, "Let's go inside and grab a cup of coffee while they fuel us."

The two started walking.

"Where's Bob?"

"Sleeping. I didn't have the heart to wake him."

"What exactly is going on?"

"You know as much as we do. Riley's missing. There were signs of a struggle on the boat but no note, call, or ransom demand. Nothing. The cops found the delivery drivers for the ship's provisioner. Both were dead in the back of the truck, which was parked in the marina parking lot. Bob called a buddy at the FBI, but all he got in return was a courtesy call."

"So where are we going?"

"Bob thinks if there will be a ransom demand, they'll call New Jersey, so that's our destination."

They walked into the warm boarding lounge of the fixed-base operator. Michaels stepped up to the counter.

"Hi. I'm 69JB."

As he suspected, the woman at the desk was in her late forties, overweight, and wearing too much makeup. "Hi. We'll have you out of here in ten minutes. Can I get a credit card from ya? I'll run it now, so you won't have to wait."

Michaels opened his wallet and placed his card on the counter.

"I'll be right back." Turning away from the counter, he smiled.

Brian caught his expression. As the two men walked out of earshot, he asked, "Let me guess. Not as cute as she sounds on the radio, right?"

Michaels shot him a look.

"It's a cop thing."

"I'm gonna hit the head, grab some coffee, and we're outta here." Michaels walked off, shaking his head, thinking Brian and Bob were too much alike.

When he returned, Brian had three cups of coffee in his hands.

"Still take it black?" Brian asked.

"Yeah. How the hell do you remember that shit?"

"It's a cop thing."

"One-hundred seventy nine and eight-tenths gallons for you tonight. Here's your receipt. Y'all stop back and see us sometime," the woman said.

Michael signed the receipt, placing one copy in his wallet. "We'll see y'all now."

As they approached the aircraft, Michaels kicked the chock from the front tire and checked the fuel caps. Brian walked toward the air-stair door. As he started up, Bob met him at the doorway.

"Hey, Dude," Brian said. "Got you some coffee."

Bob backed into the cabin, allowing Brian to climb up out of the wind, and took one of the cups. Bob settled into one of the club seats, as Brian sat in the other.

"How ya doin', Man?" Brian asked.

"Hangin' in there." Bob cleared his throat.

"Keith briefed me. Whatever you need."

"I know. I just don't understand why we haven't heard anything yet."

"You know the deal. Remember that case I worked years back? The interstate kid thing with the illegal alien parents who wouldn't call the cops, because they thought they'd be deported? They grabbed up those kids and didn't make a ransom demand for a month."

"This isn't like that. That was about drug turf."

"Yeah, well, whatever it is, I'm in."

Michaels bounded up the boarding step. "It's friggin' freezing out there."

"Drink this." Brian handed him his coffee.

"I'll take it to go." Smiling, he turned to close the cabin door. After making sure it was secure, he carried his cup to the cockpit.

"You guys can hang out back here," he said. "We'll be in

Atlantic City in a little over one hour. You got a car there?"

"Yeah," Bob said.

"All right. We should be in the bar by nine-thirty or so. Call and let 'em know you're coming if you want. Use the SAT phone. Dial country code 011, followed by the area code and number."

Michaels pulled on his headset and started reading the before-start checklist. He was worried about his friend and about Riley, whom he'd known almost as long as Bob. He was at their wedding and couldn't imagine how he'd feel if his wife went missing.

All that went through his mind while he tried to focus on flying. As he pressed the *Start* button, he focused on the inter-turbine temperature gauge carefully, and all other thoughts vanished. It was his world, where he was home. For the next hour and a few minutes, he was in control.

"They're coming! They're coming!" One of KSM's guard's excited voices echoed through the Great House and into the Great Room upstairs.

The top floor of the Great House was a 2,500 square foot playroom, complete with pool table wet bar, flatscreen TV, and plenty of plush sofas and lounge chairs. It featured floor-to-ceiling windows on three sides, offering a spectacular view. One side housed a structural wall in which the staircase from below emerged.

Hadan excused himself from KSM and turned to his journalist guests. "I want you to arrange a live feed in one hour. I want to be on the air at exactly 10:00 PM Eastern Standard Time. I've made some notes. This is what you must say. Don't reveal our location. I'll make our public demands. You'll remain on the air until I tell you to sign off. Read this. I'll return shortly."

He handed a page of notes to Padma, who read them quickly.

"Is the uplink ready?" Hadan asked.

"All ready," Mohesh said.

"Good. Set up your camera facing that wall. Place a chair in front of it and remove that picture." He nodded toward the painting on the wall. "I don't want any visible signs that might be identified from outside. Do you understand?" He glared at the cameraman.

"Yes, I understand." He didn't return the man's stare.

Confident the journalists understood their instructions, Hadan walked down to the dock as Rushi and Akshay approached. They whooped and hollered to the guards as if they had just won the World Cup, though they instantly settled down when they saw Hadan approach.

Riley was fully awake, sitting on the deck, still wrapped in plastic. Her butt was sore from sitting in the same position for hours, and the circulation in her limbs was restricted enough that her hands and feet fell asleep.

Rushi and Akshay climbed off the boat and stood before Hadan.

"You both have done a fine job," Hadan said. "Your families will be proud of you. Did all go as planned?"

"Yes, Sir." Akshay deliberately avoided eye contact.

"Good. Go up to the Great House and get cleaned up. We have much to do."

"Thank you, Sir," Rushi mumbled, keeping his head down and hoping no one noticed his swollen black eye.

As the two scrambled past Hadan and walked toward the house, Akshay tried hard not to limp. Hadan noticed everything but chose to ignore the wounds the boys displayed. They did what he asked, and that was good enough.

Hadan stepped down into the boat and bent at the waist to glare at Riley. Almost nose-to-nose, he asked, "Do you know who I am?" His tone suggested she might.

"Ahhh, let me see. I know. Hy-am?"

Hadan struggled to understand who she had him confused with.

"Hy-am, the goat fucker, right?" She gave him a huge Cheshire grin, fully expecting a violent response. She knew if her captors wanted her dead, she'd already be dead. There was little risk of retaliation.

It took him a moment to process the words from the insolent female, then he backhanded her across the face. "Silence, you arrogant bitch!"

Riley spat blood from her ruptured lip and faced him again. "You hit like a girl." She deliberately dragged out the last word, glaring at him as if he stared into a mirror. There was no fear or intimidation in her eyes, just anger.

Hadan hadn't expected that. He thought they'd have a beaten, quivering bowl of Jell-O instead of a defiant superbitch with attitude.

"Take her to the house," he snapped to the stunned guards.

"Get her cleaned up. We have work to do."

Riley wasn't going easily. The guards wrestled her from the boat and lay her on the deck. One grabbed her wrapped feet, the other her upper torso, mindful to keep themselves away from her teeth.

Hadan stood and watched them carry her off. She wasn't what he expected—not at all.

Keith greased the airplane onto the runway at Atlantic City. Running late due to weather and traffic was nothing new to Michaels, but Bob was out of his seat and squatting at the door, waiting until he could open it. As soon as the engine shut down, Bob bolted from the plane. A lineman brought his car from the parking lot, and Michaels looked out the cockpit window to see Bob already talking on his Blackberry.

Brian stuck his head into the cockpit.

"Everything good?" Michaels asked without looking up, busily completing the shutdown checklist.

"I don't know. He's checking in with the bar to see if there's been any news. I think we're gonna head there for a while."

"I'll be done here in five minutes. Try to keep him from leaving without me."

"Will do." Brian bounced down the steps after Bob.

A few minutes later, all three men were in Bob's car, heading toward The Turban.

"No news?" Michaels asked.

"No," Bob said. "Nothing. I don't get it."

"You want to call your buddy at the Fee-Bees again? Maybe he'll take your call."

"I don't know what's up with that, either. The more I think about it, the more I question the response."

Michaels, not in law enforcement like the other two, had no idea what was normal and what wasn't.

"I don't like it either," Brian said. "It's almost like he was stalling for time before answering."

"So a courtesy call isn't normal?" Michaels asked a question the other two had already figured out.

"No. Not at all."

Traffic was heavy, so it took nearly an hour to make a twenty-minute trip. As the men arrived at the bar, they saw news vans lining the street. Less than a block away, local police cars sat with their lights on.

As Bob studied the scene, his cell phone rang. Almost simultaneously, Michael's Blackberry rang. Both answered their phones.

"Where are you?" Pancho asked.

"About a block away," Bob answered. "Why?"

"I guess the local news channels in Florida figured out who Riley is. When it hit the *Associated Press* wire, the local Jersey media got hold of it. It's kind of a circus here. You want me to tell them anything?"

"Tell them I'll be there in fifteen minutes." Bob hung up and turned onto a small side street that attached to the alley behind the bar. Stopping the car, he turned to Brian.

"Give me three minutes to get in the back door, then pull back out onto the street, park, and walk in through the front door. Some of those guys might know the car, and they'll be sitting at the front door. They won't know you."

"All right," Brian said. "See ya in a few minutes."

Bob jumped out and sprinted down the alley. Brian got out of the passenger seat and ran to the driver's door. Michaels, still holding his phone to his ear, hopped into the passenger seat. It was the proverbial Chinese fire drill.

"The news is reporting Riley's disappearance as an abduction," Deborah excitedly told Michaels. "There was a murder, too. The food delivery guys were found dead near the boat. Do you know about this?"

"Yeah, we know all about it."

"What's going on?"

"Deb, you know what we do. No ransom calls, nothing. We're at The Turban. It's crawling with reporters. Brian and I will park the car and get inside. I know you're upset but can I call you back later?"

"What will you do?"

"I have no idea. Whatever Bob wants."

"Just be careful."

"Yes, Mom."

"Don't 'Yes, Mom,' me. I don't want you hurt."

"I'm with Brian and Bob. I won't be the one who gets hurt."

"Just be careful...."

He cut her off in midsentence. "I get it. Let me call you

back."

"OK. 'Bye."

Michaels hung up and saw Brian grinning at him.

"What are you grinning at?"

"Nothing, Man. I got the same speech before I left for the airport."

"We need to park this thing and go inside."

"Good plan." Brian was happy to change the subject.

They parked and walked down the block, pushing past the crowd of reporters and satellite trucks, until they entered the front door. The place was packed. Everyone was watching the ten o'clock news, which featured a story about Riley's abduction.

Pancho saw the two men walk in and signaled them toward the office. When they arrived, the door opened, and they stepped in. The tiny office was a tight fit for three. Two had to stand, because there was only one chair.

Closing the door, they heard the audio from the TV over the desk. Bob, who was on the phone, pointed at the screen, hung up, and punched speaker phone.

"Are you watching this?"

"What channel do I want?" Bob asked loudly because of the speakerphone.

"Put on the Fox News Channel."

Bob grabbed the remote and pressed a few buttons.

"This is a Fox News Alert," a newscaster said. "We're following a developing story out of Palm Beach, Florida. Earlier today, local authorities reported that Emily Riley Smith-Hershey, the noted Whitbread and Americas Cup racer, and the wife of retired Captain Robert Hershey of the New Jersey State Police, was abducted.

"Captain Hershey was the subject of a Congressional hearing following a traffic stop he made before the Giants Stadium bombing attempt that killed two unknown terrorists. We're getting reports from Sky News, our UK Affiliate, that *Al Jazeera* is carrying a live feed from the abductors, who claim to be Al-Qaeda. We'll bring that to you as soon as we can."

Bob's mind was in overdrive. Brian put his back to the wall and squatted down level with Bob.

"Who's on the phone?" Michaels asked softly, to avoid triggering the voice-activated mic on the speakerphone.

"This is FBI Deputy Director Miller," a voice said. "Who am I speaking with?"

Bob gave Michaels a *please-don't-speak* look. "Director Miller, I have two of my associates in the room. No one else is here."

"Bob, please take me off speaker." Bob picked up the receiver, which automatically cut off the speakerphone. "We have a heads-up from Homeland Security on this. I guess they intercepted some intel that tipped them that something was going on. They haven't told told me what that was, but they red-flagged the file as soon as it happened. That's why you got that courtesy call. I couldn't say anything, and I didn't know anything, anyway."

"Can you tell me who *does* know something?" Bob, incredulous, worked hard to hide his disgust.

"Off-the-record?"

"Of course."

"I'll text you a phone number. It's the private line to the Deputy Director of Intelligence of the CIA. I know him pretty well. When you call, identify yourself and say nothing else. Listen to what he says."

"The Deputy Director of Intelligence for the CIA?" Bob said it out loud so his friends could hear.

"Bob, this is bigger than you think. Wait for the text, then make the call."

"Thanks." Bob didn't know what to make of the conversation. "I will." He hung up and looked at his disbelieving friends.

"Turn it up." Michaels pointed to the TV.

Bob, who was about to speak, stopped to listen.

"This is a live feed coming from our UK affiliate Sky News. A news conference is being held by operatives of Al-Qaeda. Let's see if we can listen in."

Riley appeared on the screen, sitting upright in a chair and obviously bound. A piece of duct tape covered her mouth. Beside her was Padma Rajput, handing the microphone to Hadan, who was unmasked. Behind him stood two masked guards holding automatic weapons.

Riley wore the clothes she had on when she was abducted. Her cheek was swollen from where she fell after being choloroformed, and blood was on her blouse from when Hadan backhanded her. She looked terrible but was still alive. Unlike previous Al-Qaeda videos, which were produced in Arabic for consumption by the converted,

Hadan spoke in English. His audience was American, and he wanted them to know what he said.

"Enemies of Allah, heed my words. I'm Ali Hadan. I speak to you live and in English, so there can be no misinterpretations. Al-Qaeda has grown weary of Western intervention in our affairs. The decadent Western powers have grown weak of will, while Al-Qaeda has grown strong.

"Once upon a time, America, in all her arrogance, thought she would bring the fight to Al-Qaeda and fight us on our land. You thought that would protect your homeland from feeling our wrath. Today, Al-Qaeda has brought the fight to you."

Hadan stepped closer to Riley, as the camera zoomed in. "Today, we have abducted a U.S. citizen from American soil and taken her to a foreign land, not unlike how your government took me and my brothers from our home and brought us to Guantanamo Bay. We did this to show you that no one is safe. Homeland Security is an illusion, and you are within our reach.

"If our demands aren't met, we will behead this woman just as we beheaded Jew journalist Daniel Pearl."

Hadan drew a large sword from its sheath and placed it under Riley's throat.

The camera zoomed in to get a close-up of her face, then pulled back. The move was choreographed for maximum effect.

"Our demands will be made public in due time. I call on all the followers of Allah to stand now and rise against the West. This is your time. Allah is great!"

The camera switched to Padma, who spoke next. The live

audio was muted, and the talking heads at the news station began speaking.

"Holy fuck." Brian was shocked.

Bob pushed the *Mute* button on the remote, and noise from the bar reverberated through the tiny office.

"Where the fuck are they keeping her?" Bob mumbled, speaking for the first time since seeing his wife bound and gagged.

"What?" Michaels looked at him.

"Where are they?" He stared into Michaels' eyes.

"Shit, Man, it's been nearly twenty-four hours. They could be almost anywhere."

Bob's Blackberry rang. Looking at the screen, he saw the caller ID was EM. "It's her!"

"Wait!" Brian grabbed his hand. "It's from her phone, but it's not from her. Put it on speaker."

Bob took a deep breath and complied, setting the Blackberry on his desk. "Riley?"

"No, not Riley." The voice was ominous, like Darth Vader with a Middle Eastern accent. "This is Hadan."

"Who?" Bob, playing for time, wondered what he should say.

"Don't play the fool with me, Captain Hershey. I'm sure you know exactly who I am."

"Let me speak to my wife." His emotions got the best of him, and it took all his willpower not to lose control.

"I think not, Captain Hershey. If you ever want to see your wife alive again, I suggest you do exactly what we tell you to do."

Bob took a deep breath.

"Captain Hershey, you have caused us a great deal of trouble. You'll undo that damage by helping us avenge the deaths of our brothers and usher in a new era of fear, death, and destruction to your country. You'll help us complete the task you opposed before. Do this, and your wife lives. Disobey, and you guarantee her death."

"What exactly do you want me to do?"

"First, pay a ransom for your wife of fifty million dollars. We know your family history and know you have the money."

"Is that what this is about? Money?"

"No. That is to compensate the families you've caused great shame. The money is for them. Because we know how much the West values money, we ask for it, and that causes you shame. More importantly, we have operatives in the United States. They're being watched by your Homeland Security, but they aren't watching you. We want you to secure a van, ammonium nitrate, and diesel fuel and bring it to them. Our soldiers of the *jihad* will do the rest."

"Oh, is that all?" Bob's face turned red. "Fifty million, a van, and some fertilizer?" Veins in his neck pulsed. He exercised all the self-control he could muster.

"There's more. You'll undoubtedly be asked for an interview. You'll go on the television and will plead with your government to comply with our demands, denounce the government's aggression in our affairs, and demand that the Western powers support your government's efforts to comply. You'll do all those things."

"That's it?"

"Yes. Do you understand, Captain Hershey?"

Bob rubbed his eyes under his glasses. "I have one question."

"What is that?" Hadan's tone was deadly serious.

"Do you want fries with that global policy shift, the van, and the fifty million, or will a note from the Secretary of State and a cashier's check do?"

Hadan didn't understand. "What is this fries?"

"You're asking me to affect a change in the U.S. government's foreign policy, as if I could actually do that, with a side order of fifty million dollars and a van full of ammonium nitrate. You say it like you were ordering a meal from a fast-food joint, so I gotta know. Do you want large fries or small fries with that order?"

"You don't take this seriously, Captain Hershey. You mock me even when you hold your wife's life in your hands. Do you think this is a joke? Perhaps I should send her to you one piece at a time!" He shouted angrily into the phone.

"Don't piss him off, Dude," Michaels whispered.

Brian put a hand on Michaels' shoulder. "Hush. He knows what he's doing."

"I don't take this seriously?" Anger increased in Bob's voice. "Oh yeah, I take it seriously. You want to make this personal? Well, congratulations. You succeeded. Now let me tell you what. I won't help you do shit." He pointed at the phone as if the man could see him. "In fact, I'll make you my personal pet project, my life's mission and purpose for being. I figure for fifty million there must be some towel heads I can buy off. All I need is one of them to give you up, and your ass is mine. If anything happens to my wife, you can rest assured I'll spend the rest of my life and all of my money to kill you, your kids, your wives, and your favorite goat, too."

"Enough!" Hadan barked. "You're a big talker, a John Wayne type, eh? This is no movie, Captain. This is real. You have seventy-two hours, or you can watch your wife's execution on live TV!"

The connection went dead. Bob sat silently for what seemed a long time, though it was only seconds, then, without speaking, he stood and reached for the door.

"Wait. Where are you going?" Brian asked.

"I'm going to kill that cocksucker, that's where I'm going."

Brian put his hand against the door to keep it shut. "Dude, calm down and think it through. We don't even know where he is yet. Let's call in some favors and get some intel, then we can come up with a plan."

Bob, though he was overwhelmed with emotion and adrenalin, knew his friend was right. He slowly sat back in his chair, took a long, slow breath, and exhaled, staring into space.

"I spent my entire professional career dealing with shitbirds like this," Bob said. "They have no rules, no laws. He's just another gangbanger in a turban."

"You're right. If we can find him, we can handle it the same way, but we gotta know where to look first."

Brian spoke like a cop.

The message light on Bob's Blackberry sounded, and he saw a seven-digit phone number appear.

"This must be the DDI's number," Bob said.

"Call him," Michaels said.

Bob highlighted the number and pressed the *Call* button.

"Yes?"

"This is Bob Hershey."

"Not on the phone. Be at the Lincoln Memorial at six o'clock in the morning. Buy a *Washington Post* at the newsstand at the southwest corner. Sit on the top step facing the National Mall reflecting pool. Be alone." The call ended.

"What's up with all the cloak-and-dagger shit?" Michaels asked.

"Don't know, but...."

Someone knocked on the door.

"Enter," Bob said.

Pancho stuck her head in. "There's a shitstorm of press out here looking for you. Are you here?"

Bob considered that. "Tell them I'll be out to make a statement in thirty minutes. Can you find us some coffee? It's gonna be a long night."

"You got it, Boss. Anything else?"

"Yes. Can you hang onto Chance for a few more days? I think I gotta go out of town."

"Sure. It's kinda nice to have a man around the house. That it?"

"Yeah. I'll let you know."

"Got it." Flashing him a big grin, she closed the door behind her.

Keith and Brian stared at him.

"It's a long, sad story," Bob said. "You don't want to know."

Brian's cell phone rang. He always carried a separate cell phone for work and another for personal calls. "Hey, Cock Smear, whatta ya got?"

Michaels raised an eyebrow without speaking. Bob noticed and motioned him to lean over so he could explain.

"It's a cop thing," Bob whispered. "That's his lead detective, Doug Rodgers. The guy got drunk one night and put K-Y all over his dick then rubbed it against Brian's office door, which is made of glass. When Brian came in the next day, he was so pissed, he had a state forensics team do a crime-scene workup. Doug fessed up. Brian forgave him and nicknamed him Cock Smear. It sorta stuck."

Michaels stared at him as if it were a hidden-camera show.

"Hey, you can't make this shit up," Bob said with a smirk.

"No, I suppose not." Michaels shook his head. For a moment, Bob was entertained by the reaction of a friend who wasn't "on the job."

"Right. 'Bye." Brian snapped shut the cell phone. "Cock Smear has a good buddy at Homeland Security who's pretty high up the food chain. He wants to know if you want him to call in a favor and see if he knows anything."

"Yeah, Man. Right now, we don't know shit."

"What did the spook say?"

"Six AM at the Lincoln Memorial. How long will that take in the Pilatus?" He glanced at Michaels.

"Thanks to 9/11, we can't go to Regan. I can take you to Dulles, and it's a twenty-minute cab ride from there. At five-thirty AM there shouldn't be any traffic. It's less than an hour from Atlantic City." He might not speak cop, but he sure spoke flying. "All right. Let's go to my house, grab a shower, and get some sleep. It's nearly midnight. We gotta be at the airport by four. What will you tell the press?"

"I'm gonna play stupid. They don't know we got that call. Right now, they think they know what we know. Let's leave it at that."

"What about the demands?"

"We're playing for time."

"I hope you know what you're doing." Michael's stopped himself midsentence.

Bob knew the consequences if he guessed wrong.

As the three men left the bar, members of the press engulfed them.

"Captain Hershey! Can you tell us why you think they targeted your wife?"

Dozens of reporters shouted questions simultaneously. Cameramen tripped over each other. The glare of the lights was blinding. Bob led his buddies through the mob until they were in the middle of the street. He stopped and turned toward the mob, raising his hands to quiet them.

"Here's my statement. I know what you know. I watched it on the same TV. We have to wait and see what they want when they make their public demands. That's all I have to say for now." He turned and walked away.

"How does it feel to be targeted by the very group you helped arrest, Captain?"

Bob promised himself he wouldn't be baited into a confrontation with the press, but he was tired, and his willpower was waning. He stopped, turned, and caught himself. "How do I feel? Who are you? Dr. Phil?"

Bob turned toward the car again, proud that he hadn't given them a sound bite to replay endlessly on the news trailers.

Behind him, other reporters snickered. Brian and Keith already had the car running when Bob got in. The sea of reporters parted, as they left the parking lot.

"Bri, watch and make sure none of these numbnuts are following us."

"I'm on it."

CHAPTER SIX

Hadan turned to Riley, who was still tied to the chair. He was alone with her in the room. He didn't want witnesses to the phone call he just made.

"Your husband is a difficult man."

Riley followed him with her eyes, as he paced before her. She heard only half the conversation but could guess what Bob said.

"I'll need you to help convince him to cooperate. Your life depends on it."

Riley's mouth was still taped shut. Hadan reached down and yanked the duct tape from her mouth. The violent action reopened the split in her lip, and it began bleeding again.

"Let me guess," she said. "He told you to go fuck yourself, right?" She emphasized the word *fuck,* followed with her Cheshire grin.

"You'll do as I say, or I'll kill you myself." He bent over to get in her face. They locked eye-to-eye. Hadan couldn't understand why millions feared him, but that bitch of a woman was unaffected. The stare lasted a few seconds.

Finally, Riley said softly, "He's going to kill you. You know that, don't you?" She spoke as if telling a secret to a friend or explaining to a six-year-old that there really wasn't a Santa Claus.

"Guards!" Hadan barked.

Two guards scrambled up the steps.

"Take this bitch to her room. Tie her to her bed. Make sure she's as uncomfortable as possible."

Riley played a dangerous game, but, so far, she was winning. She knew what happened to Daniel Pearl. Frightened and angry, she made a conscious decision to channel her anger. They wanted her to show fear, to plead and beg for her life.

There was no chance she'd give them what they wanted, just because they wanted it. She heard the phone call and knew Bob hadn't reacted as anticipated.

She also knew she had seventy-two hours to live.

Three exhausted men climbed out of the cab in front of the Lincoln Memorial at five minutes before six in the morning. The sky was still dark but starting to lighten, and it was bitter cold.

"You two get lost for about fifteen minutes. I'll call your cell phone when I'm done."

"You sure about this?" Michaels sounded concerned.

"Yeah. What's he gonna do to me?"

"Good point. Come on. I'll buy ya a cup of coffee." Michaels and Brian walked away.

Bob turned toward the newsstand. "*Washington Post,* please."

The man handed him a newspaper. Bob paid him a dollar, tucked the paper under his arm, and bounded up the monument steps. Wind blew through the pillars like a wind tunnel, making an eerie sound. Bob sat on the top step, facing the Reflecting Pool, as the sun lightened the horizon. The silhouette of the Capitol at the opposite end of the mall was breathtaking.

He wasn't there more than sixty seconds before a voice spoke behind him. "Please don't turn around, Mr. Hershey."

Bob complied.

"Please turn the crossword page, if you don't mind."

When Bob did, a 9x12 unmarked envelope fell from between the pages. He picked it up and began opening it.

"Your wife is being held on an island in the Bahamas," the voice said. "In that envelope are infrared images shot from a Global Hawk less than an hour ago."

Bob took out the photos and studied them.

"Our best assessment is that there are fifteen or sixteen hostiles. Most are armed with light-to-medium automatic weapons, AKs, we think. There's a news crew there from *Al-Jazeera*. They established a satellite link, so they can send a live feed from that location."

"Go on." Bob recognized an intelligence briefing when he heard one.

"As far as we can tell, Ali Hadan and Kalid Sheik Mohammed are physically on-site. Their profiles are in that envelope."

"What do they want with my wife?"

"It has nothing to do with your wife, Mr. Hershey. They

chose her because of your involvement with the Giants Stadium bombing incident."

"Yeah, but what do they really want?" Annoyed, Bob wanted to know why her.

"Go home and turn on your TV. News of this abduction has sparked riots throughout Europe. This is what the Europeans feared most—an event that would galvanize the Muslim world behind the extremists. This will spread to North Africa and the Middle East as the day passes. Pro-Western Muslim nations like Turkey will be threatened. It's all a grand publicity stunt to show the West what kind of power they can wield and that they can operate in the open with impunity. They're trying to gain legitimacy on the world stage. It has nothing to do with your wife. She was just a convenient target."

"What's the government going to do about it?" He didn't want to be part of a charade.

"Nothing."

"Nothing? How can they justify doing nothing?"

"This comes right from the top, Mr. Hershey, directly from the White House. Their policy is not to give the event any credibility. They're afraid doing so would trigger a panic in the States. Can you imagine what would happen if people thought they could be snatched off the street in front of their houses? There would be anarchy."

"But they can. That's exactly what happened. If the government knows where these people are, why not send in a SEAL team to take them out and get my wife back?" His voice rose.

"We don't have that kind of political reciprocity with the Bahamas. They won't sanction military action on their own soil.

We've been specifically ordered not to engage in any Black Ops, either. Apparently, the State Department thinks this can be negotiated, like the Somali pirate situation a few years ago."

"Forgive me if memory fails, but didn't that situation end up with mass casualties?" He knew he was right but wanted to make a point.

"Yes, but they were French casualties, not American. The Somali government sanctioned military action by a third-party nation. That isn't the case here. I guess, in their minds, they don't want your wife's death on their watch."

Bob tried to process the information as fast as his mind allowed. "Why are you telling me this?" He wasn't sure if he should be angry or start crying.

"Because, Mr. Hershey, my boss disagrees with the administration's position, but his hands are tied. When I told him you might be the only man in the country to be fucked by his government three times in one lifetime, he agreed to look the other way and allow me to pass this intel to you."

"Do I know you?" He tried to find a connection.

"Yes, Mr. Hershey, you do. I had the distinct dishonor of running you out of the Army. I thought you got a raw deal then, and I also thought you got a raw deal at that farce of a Congressional hearing. I think you're getting a raw deal right now. Look, I can't promise anything. This conversation never happened, but, if I can support you with intel, I'll try to help."

"Captain Kirk?" Bob's eyes widened as he turned quickly to face his former nemesis. Kirk had aged badly. Bob wouldn't have recognized him if he hadn't identified himself. Their eyes locked for a moment.

"Why are you helping me now?"

"Go get your wife, Mr. Hershey. No one else will do it for you." Kirk turned and bolted into the shadows of the Memorial.

Bob stood there, stunned, his mind awash in information, flooded with emotion, and tempered with exhaustion. He paused to look at the material in the envelope. It contained latitude and longitude, satellite recon photos, Infer-red aerial photos showing guards' positions and people asleep, lists of radio frequencies, threat-assessment reports, and a ton of other useful information.

He quickly closed the documents in the newspaper and took the steps down two at a time. Minutes later, he and his friends were in a cab on their way back to the airport.

"You guys won't believe this," Bob said, as the cab door closed.

Four hours later, they landed in Palm Beach. Bob and Brian spent the entire flight poring over the intel Kirk gave them while making a few calls on the SAT phone.

"Let's get something to eat," Bob told Michaels, as he went down the boarding ramp. "Brian and I have a plan."

"Plan?" Michaels realized how tired he was. He paused to install the gust lock on the plane's yoke and followed Bob toward the fixed-base operator's office.

Once they had a table in the pilot's lounge, Bob spread out the photos. "OK. Here's what we got. They've got Riley on this island."

Michaels looked at the aerial photo. "That's Musha Cay!"

"How do you know?" Bob asked, surprised.

"I flew charter down there for seven years. My company ran a Twin Otter that supported the island for years. I've been there a hundred times."

Bob looked stunned.

"Hey, it's a pilot thing. Ya can't make this stuff up." Michaels said with a smug expression. For the first time in two days, he was ahead of the conversation.

"You have to be shitting me." Bob didn't believe it.

"I shit you not. I know that place pretty well. Is that where they've got Riley?"

"Yeah."

"Go on." Michaels, enjoying being ahead of the curve, motioned with his hand to continue.

"The intel shows the guards are posted to protect from an approach from the water. They're all around the shoreline. See?" He pointed at the light-colored silhouettes on the infrared photos. "There are no guards, however, on the island's interior."

"Interior?" Michaels asked. "That rock's only a mile long and half a mile wide. What interior?"

"Let me finish, please." Bob raised his eyebrows, universally known as a bad sign to anyone who knew him.

Michaels shut up. His smugness faded. Bob was in full tactical-brief mode, something he did a thousand times in his career.

"Brian and I figure we can jump in and land in this field. It's large enough." He pointed at one photo. "I need you to drop us from at least 10,000 feet, so they won't hear us coming. Then I need you to land on this airstrip on the island next door."

"That's Rudder Cut Cay."

Bob's eyebrows went up again. "Brian and I will grab Riley and make our way down to these docks. There are at least two boats in this photo and a couple jet skis. See these light spots? Those are the motors' heat signatures. I need you to cover our egress from the other side and fly us out of there."

"Cover you how?"

"I'll give you my Remington 70. It's equipped with a night-vision scope, but try not to shoot us in the process."

"Are you kidding? Do I look like Lee Harvey Oswald to you? I haven't shot a long gun in twenty years, and you never jumped from a plane in your life. You're gonna hit a drop zone in the dark?"

The conversation was becoming heated.

"Brian and I will tandem jump. He was night-qualified High Altitude Low Opening in the Marines."

"We can get a big tandem chute that we can control with a high degree of accuracy," Brian added, only to be cut off by Michaels, who was clearly animated.

"Dude, are you nuts? That was thirty-five years ago! Look in the mirror, Guys. We're a bunch of fifty-somethings. We qualify for a Flomax commercial, not a Rambo movie."

"There's more," Bob said.

"Oh, goody. Do tell."

"You have to do this dead stick, with NVGs, or they'll see or hear you."

"You've gotta be kidding. Drop you two out of a plane, then dead-stick land on a dirt strip in the middle of the ocean in pitch darkness wearing night-vision goggles, shoot a moving target 300 yards away with a weapon I haven't fired in twenty years, then fly us all out? Anything else?"

"We need to do it with a minimal radar profile. Intel shows they have radar, but we can't tell if it's for boats or planes."

Michaels looked at Brian, who was silent throughout most of the exchange. "Say something, Brian. This is crazy."

Agitated, Michaels stood and paced. Bob was serious. He thought the mission through and had a way in and out. Brian's only comment was about the chute.

Michaels and Bob exhausted all their arguments, and a pregnant silence filled the room. Brian, finally leaning forward in his Lazy Boy, looked straight at Michaels.

"Keith, if it was Debbie, he'd be going, and I'd be going. What else do you need to know?"

Michaels, overwhelmed by the seriousness of the task, exhaled loudly and sank into his chair, rubbing his eyes. Brian and Bob waited.

Michaels knew all the arguments. It was one of those put-up-or-shut-up moments. There was no way to say no, to say he had a wife and kids, because so did the others. Declining would end a lifetime of friendship and commitment from the only two men on earth who would help if it was his wife, not Bob's.

"You two are insane. You know that, right? This might be a

suicide mission."

They stared at him.

"Damn it, I'm in, but please can we try this once before doing it for real? I'd like to try those NVGs once, since I've never used them before. There are a million logistical issues, too."

Bob and Brian looked relieved.

"Like what?" Bob asked.

"Well, like crossing the Air Defense Intercept Zone for one. We need to file a flight plan, or we're gonna be explaining ourselves to a pair of F-16s. Then we have to figure out how to get all your toys to the Bahamas. We can't exactly clear customs with a Remington 70 onboard."

"What can we use for a plane?" Bob asked.

"Good question. I can borrow a Maule M-5 from a customer. It's mostly tube and fabric, so it won't show up on radar very well. It gets in and out at about 600 feet, and it has a double-wide cargo door on the back we can remove and still fly, so you can jump. It'll be slow and noisy, but it'll still fly.

"It has a good GPS system in it, so I can use that to calculate the wind speed and direction for the drop, then line up for that postage stamp of a runway on Rudder Cut. How much stuff will we need to carry in pounds?"

"I'm not sure. No more than, maybe, one-hundred seventy-five to two-hundred pounds. Why?"

"Because the plane is weight-limited. We can carry fuel, or we can carry stuff, but not both." He rubbed his eyes, unable to believe he was having such a conversation. "Technically, it's doable, but I can't account for things I don't know that I don't know."

"Like what?"

"Like what happens if someone puts a bullet through the fuel tank, or what the speed and fuel burn will be without the door on the plane. It's a long way down there and back, without many places to stop along the way."

"If we do this right, they won't even know we're there. They won't expect us. We'll have the element of surprise."

"Yeah, but you don't know which one of those little white dots is Riley." He pointed at the infrared photo.

"I can make an educated guess," Bob said.

"Dude, it's your ass out there. You need to guess right."

"Don't you think I know that?" Bob snapped.

"Sorry, Man. I know you know, but this is right out of the Ross Perot playbook."

Michaels referred to the rescue of billionaire Ross Perot's employees from Iran during the Iranian hostage crisis. In 1979, two of Perot's employees were taken hostage by the Iranian government. When the U.S. government refused to take action, Perot directed a successful rescue mission executed by his own employees and led by retired Green Beret Colonel Arthur "Bull" Simons. Perot went to Iran and entered the prison where his men were held. Ken Follett wrote a bestselling novel, *On Wings of Eagles,* about the event.

"Yeah, and they did it with a handful of computer nerds, not two career cops. This can work!"

"Shit, Man, I hope so." Michaels fell back into his Lazy Boy.

"I can get Cock Smear to bring us the hardware. He'll charter a plane and be here tonight," Brian said. "He's trying to get additional intel from his DHS buddy."

"Great. Look, it's 11:30. I need to go home, round up this plane, and do some math. I'm probably gonna have to rig a jump step or something so you two don't hit the tail on the way out. We can try it later tonight, like around eleven. We can fly out to Airglades, a remote agricultural strip on the west side of Lake Okeechobee. No one lives out there. We can try this out and see if we kill ourselves. Are we up for that?" He hoped they wouldn't resist a practice run.

"Yeah, good," Brian answered for Bob.

"Brian, you get on the phone and find us a chute. I'll take care of the hardware." Bob snapped back into state-police-captain mode.

"If the practice jump goes well, here's what I propose," Michaels continued. "I say we fly out of here in the morning and land at the old Georgetown airport. No one goes there anymore. It's been abandoned since they built the new one, but it was never officially decommissioned. The runway's a mess, but it's certainly usable.

"We ditch our gear, fly to the new airport, and clear customs. There's no radar out there, at least no air-traffic-control radar, so no one will know we stopped. On the way down, we'll be on a legitimate flight plan. I recommend we overfly Musha and take some digital pictures to get a good look from about 1,500 feet. We get a motel room, look at the pictures, and maybe get some sleep. We drive to the old strip to get our gear. There's no night flying in the Bahamas, not VFR, anyway. If we leave in the dark, and someone hears us, they might report us to the Civil Aviation Authorities, but Musha's only twenty-five miles. We'll be climbing the whole time to altitude. They won't have time to do anything before we're on our way down again. The only thing I'm not sure of is if our friends on Musha have anyone watching the airport at Mosstown for anything unusual."

"Let me think about that," Bob said. "Let's meet at the airport at ten o'clock to try this."

"Yeah. Ten PM at my hangar. See ya there." Michaels walked for the door, his mind racing. As he settled into his car, he took out his cell phone and pushed auto dial.

"Hey, are you back?" Deborah asked. "What's up with Riley?"

"I'm on the way home. Wanna have lunch with your husband?"

"Sure. I'm at my mother's house. I'll be home in an hour. Wait for me."

"See ya in an hour."

"Is everything all right?"

"Yeah. I'll tell ya about it over lunch."

"OK. Love you. 'Bye."

Selling the deal to his wife wouldn't be easy. Deciding to wing it, he shifted his attention to the task at hand and pressed another speed dial.

"Hey, Buddy," he said.

"Hey. What's up with Bob?" Matt Calloway, his longtime mechanic, asked. Calloway learned to fly from Michaels when he was just a teenager. Michaels helped him enlist in the Air Force, and, when he got out, Michaels helped him start his own aircraft-maintenance business.

"I need you to do something for me. Go to Fort Lauderdale and get Sue Roberts' Maule and bring it to the hangar. I need you to remove the cargo door and rig a jump step. Can you do that?"

"Sure I can, but why?"

"I need you to do it and not ask questions. Can you do that?"

"You want me to rig her for jumping and not ask questions?"

"Exactly."

"All right, but you're gonna need to tell me what's going on."

"Dude, please, just do this. We'll talk later."

Matt hesitated, sensing the urgency in Michaels' voice. "All right. When?"

"How about now?"

"OK. I'll head down there now. See ya at the airport later."

"Later, then."

"Is this OK with Sue?"

"I'll make it OK."

"On my way."

"'Bye." Michaels hung up.

Matt wasn't stupid. He knew something was up, but in case the operation went wrong, Michaels didn't want anyone to know more than necessary. Less than a minute later, he called Sue.

"Hi, Sue. It's Keith."

"Hi. How are you? What's going on with Bob? It's all over the news."

"I know. I just flew him down here from Jersey. He's pretty upset."

Sue Roberts was one of Keith's clients who became a true

friend. She married a child film star named David Roberts. Together, they chose to ditch the Hollywood celebrity scene and raise their kids in Florida, far from the paparazzi's prying eyes. Sue was a pilot who hadn't flown in years when she met Keith. He got her back into flying and eventually sold her the Maule, which wasn't a luxury aircraft, more the aeronautical equivalent of a Jeep. Loud and drafty with wind in the pilot's hair, it was all fun, the perfect plane for Sue's personality.

"I'll bet. Give him my love, will you?"

"Of course. Hey, can I use your plane for a day or so? I need to run out to a little strip in the Bahamas, and I need a STOL airplane like yours." The Maule was the king of Short Takeoff and Landing. "My Cessna's in for an annual inspection and is in a million pieces right now."

"Sure. You don't need to ask."

"I appreciate that, but I never want to wear out my welcome."

"That's not likely."

"How's David?"

"Doing great. He's working on a Broadway play in New York. I haven't seen him in a week."

"So much for retirement, huh?"

"Yeah, right."

He wanted the conversation to sound as normal as possible. "Hey, when I get back, I'll call, and we can do lunch or something."

"That would be great. We can fly somewhere cool for lunch."

"Sounds like a plan. See ya."

"See ya."

Michaels knew that the plane's registration number would bring the mission back at Sue if it went badly. For her own good, she couldn't know about it.

All he had left was to sell this fiasco to his wife.

Thirty minutes later, Keith stood before the full-length mirror in his bedroom, zipping up the front of his ancient Nomex flight suit, amazed it still fit. He carefully let out the straps on the shoulder harness for his handgun and slid the pistol into its holster.

"Wow," he muttered. "Not bad." He was still admiring himself when Debbie walked into the room.

"High, Hon." She froze in midstep. "What's going on?"

"Look, Deb...." Trying to figure out what to say, he sat on the edge of the bed. "We know where Riley is. She's on Musha Cay in the Bahamas. The government won't do anything about it."

"How do you know that?"

"We know."

"Yeah? What do you think you're going to do about it?" Whenever she was angry, her Long Island accent came out.

"Bob wants to go get her. Brian's going with him. They asked me to fly the plane."

"Are you fucking nuts? Are you watching the news? This is an international event, not a celebrity charter to the Bahamas!"

"Yeah, I know, but it's Riley. They'll kill her—on TV. This isn't like it's someone we don't know."

"Why are you wearing a gun?" She didn't wait for an answer.

"There's no way you're doing this." Tears filled her eyes.

"Hey, wait...."

"No, Keith. Don't, 'Hey, wait,' me. We waited till Matthew went to college, so we could have some quality time together. You aren't going off to get yourself killed over this!" She was hysterical.

Keith grabbed her to stop her from flailing at him.

"Don't do this!" she sobbed. "You aren't trained for this!"

"Deb, listen to me. Listen carefully. If it were you, instead of Riley, they'd go. Do you understand that? These guys spent their professional careers dealing with shit like this. They know what they're doing."

"They're cops, not commandos. You're all gonna get yourselves killed. What about Brian? What does his wife say? His kids are still in school."

"Deb, Brian's not asking, he's going. I need to do this. These are our friends. They're as close to family as you can get. There isn't anyone else. The government is pretending it didn't happen. I don't know why, but that's what it is. Believe me, I'm not happy about this. In fact, I'm scared shitless, but I can't stand by and let it happen to someone I've known as long as I've known you. I couldn't live with that."

"And if you get yourself killed? What about me?"

"First, I won't get myself killed. Second, I don't think it's a good idea for you to know too much, either, in case this thing blows up. You need to play stupid if anyone asks you anything before I return."

"What am I supposed to say?"

"Tell them your husband's a pilot, and he's out flying. That's what he does. There's nothing unusual about that, right? I'm more concerned about what happens when we return."

"Why?"

"Why? 'Cause we're gonna break about a dozen laws in two different countries. If this goes as planned, we'll come back without passports, customs notification, or ID of any kind. We'll cross the ADIZ without notification and land without an inbound notification. They get testy about shit like that."

"That's what you're worried about? Breaking some insignificant immigration laws?"

"Hey, it's Homeland Security. They make up this shit as they go. They can seize the plane, arrest the pilot, and hold him indefinitely. Shit, they don't even need to give you a lawyer."

"So what are you saying? You might save her life and end up in jail for it?"

"I don't know, but yes, that crossed my mind. A lot of stuff is in my head right now. That's why I need you behind me on this. I can't do this and worry about you simultaneously. You always had my back on everything since we were married. We ran a business, raised a kid, and we did all right. We've been partners in everything, the good and the bad. I need you to have my back on this, too."

He looked her in the eye, and she knew in her heart he was right. She couldn't live with herself if something happened to Riley and she and Keith could've done something, anything, to stop it.

"Please don't get yourself killed."

"There's no chance your next husband gets all my toys that

easily."

"I don't want a next husband. I want you." Tears filled her eyes again. "I'll sell all your shit in a New York minute if you go and get yourself killed." She forced a smile through her thinly veiled threat.

"I'm coming back."

"You'd better."

"Gimme a hug."

They were locked in each other's arms for a moment. Debbie stood to get a tissue. The explanation went better for Keith than he imagined, but the possibility of being killed became real for the first time. Until then, it was discussions about the tactically possible versus the impossible. Debbie put the possibility of death in human terms. There was a chance, no matter how small, he might not come back.

Keith didn't have a chance to say good-bye to his son. He lay on the bed and closed his eyes for a minute, thinking about what he'd say to Matthew if he could. Then he walked to the desk to write him a note, just in case. If he didn't come back, he needed his son to know the truth, not a story from some government news source.

Matthew needed to know many things, not all of which could be compressed into a single note. It took Keith over an hour to get all his thoughts down on paper. Once he finished, he carefully folded the letter and placed it in an envelope addressed to his son. He set it on his laptop, where he knew someone would find it.

Physically and mentally exhausted, his mind screamed for sleep. "It's a little past three in the afternoon," he said.

Dragging himself to the sofa, he curled up with his dog and fell asleep.

Two hours later, Debbie frantically shook him awake. "Turn on the news, quick!"

Keith, in a post-nap stupor, looked for the remote control. By the time he found a news station, Debbie was almost standing on him.

"Come on!" she said.

"Geez. What's so urgent?"

He saw scenes of civil unrest and violence from nearly every country in the world. France was under martial law. Great Britain considered doing the same. Madrid was on fire. The Turkish government was near collapse.

In the U.S., there was no violence from pro-Muslim supporters, but there were widespread public displays of support for what was happening by the American Muslim community, similar to the events after 9/11 but on a larger scale.

The President's statement from the White House called for calm and sent a warning to those who would seek retribution against the American Muslim community for events happening abroad.

"That's great," Keith said. "Instead of calling for the Muslim community to denounce this shit, he warns Americans not to seek retribution while they celebrate in the streets. What a country. You woke me up for this shit?"

"This is a big deal, Hon. You're in the middle of this shitstorm."

"I feel better about doing what we planned after seeing this. Bob will shit a chicken when he hears it. What's wrong with these people?" he asked in disgust.

Though Keith wasn't as emotional about the political climate as Bob, the situation went beyond ridiculous. He sat on the edge of the sofa, rubbing sleep from his eyes.

"I have to shower and check the weather." He snapped off the TV before walking toward the bedroom.

Bob and Brian met Cock Smear at Palm Beach International Airport. On the south side, where general aviation activity was conducted, a Lear 35 taxied onto the general aviation ramp, where Bob and Brian waited to meet it. Bob positioned his rented SUV by the air stair door. When it opened, Detective Rodgers crouched in the doorway.

"Did you get everything we asked for?" Brian asked.

"Nice to see you, too, Chief. Sorry to hear about your wife, Bob. Wish I was going with you."

"No, you don't, and you have no idea where we're going, understand?" Bob peered at him over the rim of his glasses.

"You realize that none of this stuff can come back, right? Don't worry. We have no idea what you're talking about."

Brian looked at him with his *No shit, Captain Obvious* look that most people assumed he practiced in front of a mirror.

"It's all here," Rodgers said. "Three M4A3s with ten mags each, one Benelli 12-gauge with a box of fifty rifle slugs, three V-10 45s with extra clips plus 300 rounds and three sets of NVGs. I've got twelve ounces of C-4 and two remote detonators.

"I also threw in a case of flash bangs, four vests, and tactical webbing. You know, the usual assault stuff, just in case. I got the oversized MC-4 chutes you wanted, and oh yea, I went to Bob's house and grabbed his Remington 70. Got the scope and bipod too. Now that's some nice shit."

He stopped in midsentence. The gear was packed in black canvas duffel bags and a couple hard cases. They quickly transferred the cache into the back of the SUV.

"Oh, yeah, one more thing," Rodgers said. "My buddy at DHS didn't say much, but he gave me this." He handed Brian an envelope. "They're kinda busy with a million domestic threats they didn't see yesterday. Hope it helps."

"Thanks." Brian shook his hand. "Hey, you don't know too much, understand?"

"I got it the first time, Chief. Good luck, Guys." He stepped back into the Lear, and the captain started the engines.

Bob and Brian drove toward the gate.

"Let's get out of here ASAP," Bob said. "This is an airline-served airport, with cameras everywhere."

"Got it."

Brian navigated the airport parking area toward the street, while Bob opened the envelope Rodgers gave them. It contained a classified, eyes-only DHS situation report of various domestic-threat scenarios. It included what DHS might expect domestically if Al-Qaeda went through with the threat to execute Riley on TV versus what to expect if something unplanned happened.

There were several variations, such as what would happen if Riley were tortured but released, not tortured and released, and more. There was a threat assessment of possible domestic backlash from U.S. citizens who weren't happy with Homeland Security's response to the different scenarios. The report projected a high *negative impression* of DHS and the administration's policies in particular in the event of a botched rescue attempt that resulted in *casualties*. It concluded that, based on that scenario, creating the highest possible domestic threat, no rescue attempt should be made.

Bob's blood pressure rose as he read. His face went flush. Brian had the radio playing softly and didn't pay Bob much attention.

"Dude, are you OK?" Brian finally asked.

"Brian, you have to read this."

"Why? What does it say?"

"If I told you, you'd think I was lying."

"Try me."

He took a deep breath and turned in his seat to face Brian. "It says that DHS is afraid if they attempt a rescue, and it fails, there'll be a backlash against them and the administration from Joe Public. That's why they won't try to save her."

"You're kidding, right?"

"Nope."

"You need to keep that memo in a safe place. We might need it later for leverage."

Bob's eyes widened. "You're right. They wouldn't want the media to get hold of this. You know what? Pull over into that shopping center. There's a mailbox store in there. I'll FedEx this to the bar, so it won't be on us where someone might find it."

"Good plan. Make a copy first, just in case."

"Aye-itt." Bob used his best street slang.

"Those cocksuckers! They're making domestic security decisions based on anticipated public perceptions. They don't want to look bad."

"Yeah, well, it's an election year."

"Un-fucking-believable."

"You need to stay calm and focus on the task at hand. We don't give a shit about public perception. This is just about getting the job done."

"Dude, it's not my job, it's my wife."

"Man, I'm your friend. I'm telling you that you need to look at this as a job, not something personal. Otherwise, you'll get hurt. It's like going through the door of another meth lab. A shitbird is a shitbird. It doesn't matter what he wears on his head. Got it?" Brian tried to keep Bob in law-enforcement mode and not allow his emotions to creep into his decision-making process, which might be fatal.

It was also time to change the subject. "I'm gonna get some coffee. You want any?"

"Yeah. Venti mocha frappuccino, no whip."

"Are you sure there's enough sugar in that for you?"

"It's gonna be a long night." Bob smiled for the first time all day and hopped from the car.

Bob's cell phone rang constantly. Every reporter wanted a comment from him. As he and Brian went to the airport to meet

Keith, they listened to the radio. India and Pakistan put their respective armies on alert. Secular violence in those countries threatened to ignite into war. Even under the best of circumstances, it wouldn't take much to make them shoot at each other.

In the context of secular violence generated by a well-executed publicity stunt, Al-Qaeda accomplished more than it had hoped for. They took a bold step, employing technology to spread their word. For the first time, they also ignited the passions of the extremists simultaneously.

CHAPTER SEVEN

On any other day, the veranda on the beach at Musha Cay would be an idyllic setting for a four-star meal. That night, it played host to two of the world's most-notorious terrorists. Dressed in traditional white robes and headdress, looking more like Arab royalty than terrorists, KSM and Hadan dined on Caribbean lobster and conch, prepared by a team of world-class chefs.

The two men were pleased with themselves. A few years earlier, they were locked in a four-star detention center in Cuba, eating prison food. That night, they spoke of their good fortune. They marveled at the string of good luck and seemingly coincidental events that brought them to such a place.

Both agreed they read the political gesturing of the Western countries with absolute accuracy. It was clear the West had no stomach for a long, protracted war on terror. Indeed, they stopped calling it a war. The powers in Washington wouldn't be willingly drawn into a confrontation with Al-Qaeda for fear of igniting domestic strife.

The two men mused that the leaders of Europe and pro-

Western Arab states were probably making frantic phone calls at that moment, begging the U.S. not to exacerbate the already-incendiary situation. It appeared the West would do nothing.

They gambled on that and won big. The longer they played out the situation, the longer the worldwide violence would continue. When they finally executed their captive on TV, they anticipated a crescendo of violence. A wave of hard-core sympathizers would do the same to whatever Westerner they could get their hands on. They planned their evening broadcast together, knowing the global violence they sparked would make the West amenable to any demands that would stop it.

What they didn't understand was Captain Hershey. His wife's life was at stake, yet he hadn't complied with any of their demands. There were no interviews denouncing his country, no pleas for mercy or his wife's life, and no money. Even though he was nothing more than a vendetta to them, they didn't understand his silence.

"You think like an American," KSM said. "Why haven't we heard from Captain Hershey?"

Hadan felt the remark was an insult. "He's a beaten man. He was shunned by his own kind for trying to protect his country, and it appears he can't protect his wife, either."

"Do you not expect to hear from him?"

"No. I think he has accepted the inevitable fate for his wife, and he's powerless to do anything about it. A man like Hershey doesn't take well to appearing impotent before the world."

"It would've been nice to get him to beg for her, like they begged for Daniel Pearl. That did much to rally the faithful. It would've made our success here even sweeter. What do you plan for tonight?"

"I will taunt the West and call them powerless. I'll show how they can't protect even a single woman, much less a country. I'll threaten more of the same if they don't denounce their war on terror. If they don't recognize Al-Qaeda as an entity to be negotiated with and order an immediate stand-down of U.S. armed forces everywhere in the world except on their own soil, we will act."

"Do you really expect a response?" KSM was intrigued by such bold ideas.

"No. Washington will do what it has always done—nothing. I expect we will execute our guest tomorrow night as planned. Many of Allah's faithful soldiers will do the same. I hope for an event of such magnitude that one of two things will happen.

"First, a regime change in Washington. Better yet, capitulation from the West in the form of some backdoor communication through the Saudi royal family. The West will need a way to save face, similar to the Cuban missile crisis of 1962. The Soviets agreed to remove their missiles from Cuba only after they were secretly assured through backdoor negotiations that America would remove its missiles from Turkey.

"The U.S. insisted they must wait six months to avoid any appearance of a link between the two events. In the end, the Soviets got what they wanted all along. They were far more successful than they imagined possible, because they created a permanent communist state ninety miles off the U.S. coast. From there, they could torment their adversary endlessly.

"That's what we've done here. We've created a situation from which the American people feel genuine fear. In 1962, it was nuclear war. Our situation is more insidious, because it's random, without warning, and there's no defense against it. Like the Soviets in 1962, we have little to lose and much to gain. The global reaction to our *jihad* by the faithful has been an unanticipated bonus. It has presented us with an opportunity we can't afford to squander. It will advance our cause many years."

"You've spent much time considering these possibilities. So far, you've been right."

"This is what we talked about in Cuba. We said we'd do it if given the chance. In 2001, we used their lifestyle against them. They spent fortunes to protect themselves from that threat. All it took was twenty uneducated men armed with box cutters. They spent billions each year just to prevent that. They speak of freedom, but they've surrendered it to us.

"They build fences on their borders, yet we move our drugs and people freely. They speak of Homeland Security, yet we do as we please. Their rules only apply to the law-abiding. We don't recognize their laws. It's only now that their people see this. Their money and politics can't protect them from us. Other nations have the same problem. They, too, are powerless to protect themselves, much less help the United States. We have sympathetic nation states in positions of power in the United Nations. We're this close to attaining credibility on a global scale." He held up his thumb and index finger an inch apart. He was clearly excited and animated, an unusual state for the normally stoic man.

"And military intervention?" KSM set down his fork and looked Hadan squarely in the eye.

"There's no chance of military intervention. Our people in the U.S. would alert us to even the possibility. The American administration is so fearful of a lawsuit in World Court, they'd never send troops into another sovereign nation without that nation's approval. As you know, we pretty much own the Bahamian government."

"Again, so far, you've been right."

"They don't even know where we are."

"How do you know?"

"If they did, our people would've told us. We'd see asset movement—satellite orbit changes, UAVs, something. If they knew where we were, we'd already know."

"Nonetheless, I will spend the night on the other side of the island. Perhaps that's from too many years of hiding, but I can't sleep in plain sight."

"I understand. Do you wish to attend tonight's broadcast?"

"No. I'll be there tomorrow night to do the honors."

"As you wish."

"Hadan, what have you planned for our two young reporters?"

"I'm still weighing the benefits of letting them go spread the word versus how much they know about our intelligence network. Right now, they have no knowledge of our U.S. contacts or the friendly nations assisting us with information. What happens here in the Bahamas is covered with a legitimate story that they'll undoubtedly support as the truth, because they know nothing else. If things suddenly went wrong, they might become casualties. We must wait and see."

KSM sat back in his chair, clearly not happy with the repast.

"What's the matter?" Hadan worried it might be something he said.

"I don't care much for this type of food. I long for a simple bowl of couscous." He gave a forced smile.

"Tomorrow, when the plane goes to Georgetown for supplies, I'll make sure they get the ingredients to make that for you."

"Thank you, Hadan." KSM stood.

Even those two men couldn't ignore the beauty of the moment. The sun set below the western horizon, and the clouds were illuminated in vibrant pink in a teal sky.

"It reminds one of Cuba, does it not?" KSM asked.

"I try not to think anything good about Cuba. I only want to remember how angry it made me to be held there. That's the source of my energy and focus."

"Don't let your hatred of that place blind you to the reality of today, Hadan. We still have much to do. Tomorrow will be a critical day."

"I understand."

KSM turned to leave, then paused. "Hadan, one more thing."

"Yes? What is it?"

"I want you to personally inspect the guards tonight. You say no one knows where we are, but I'm still paranoid. That's the source of my focus. That's how I managed to stay alive."

"I understand."

"You'll see to it?"

"I'll do it personally, as you requested."

"Good. *Allah Akbar.*"

"*Allah Akbar.*"

Hadan remained on the veranda, as KSM walked down the dock toward the beach. It occurred to Hadan that it was the first time since they boarded the plane in Kuwait that they were alone, out of earshot of the ever-present guards. KSM chose them himself. He knew each of them and their families. That was part of the secret to his success in a business where success was measured by survival. They were fiercely loyal to him, the equivalent of Argus, the all-seeing dog of the Greek god Zeus. Nothing went unnoticed.

As Hadan walked off the pier toward the Great House, he motioned to his guards. "Go get our guest and take her upstairs. Bring me the reporters. I will wait here."

The men scurried off without a word. Hadan needed to brief his captive news team of the upcoming broadcast and to interrogate them to determine how much they knew, but it had to be done carefully, so it wouldn't appear to be an interrogation. If they suspected, he knew they would lie.

He needed to know if they knew about the U.S. contacts and their men at *Al Jazeera*. He arranged to gain operational control of the satellite feed, so it couldn't be shut down. He couldn't risk the possibility that the people at *Al Jazeera* would run out of nerve and end his show. No one could know in advance, or they would simply reroute the uplink. His plan must remain safe.

At the Lantana airport, Michaels entered the gate and pulled up to the hangar, where Matt, Brian, and Bob were waiting. It was a typical Florida winter night, with light wind, high humidity, and the drone of training aircraft flying in the traffic pattern. Because there was no airline service at the airport, there was no manned security. The only thing to get past was a gate that required a card key and security cameras.

Michaels stepped inside to find Bob and Brian had spread out their gear on the floor. Matt leveled an M-4 at the wall.

"What the fuck are you doing?" Michaels asked.

"Relax, Dude. I was just showing Matt our toy collection."

"Christ, why don't you post it on the friggin' Internet? Twitter the whole thing, why don't you?"

"What's his problem?" Brian looked at Bob.

"My problem is, the less people who know what we're doing the better chances of success, not to mention what would happen to them when, and if, we return."

Matt lowered the M-4. "Relax. Did you really think I couldn't figure this out for myself? Rig a plane with a jump door but don't ask questions? Do you really think I'm that stupid?"

"If you're so smart, then you'd know you'd be considered a co-conspirator if charges are brought against us."

"Charges? Who's gonna charge you for saving someone's life?"

Bob and Brian stopped smiling. A long pause ensued. Matt looked at them and realized he hadn't considered the possibility of criminal charges.

"Is the plane rigged?" Michaels changed the subject.

"Yeah," Matt said. "Ready to go."

"Great. One more thing. Take a gallon of Marvel Mystery Oil off the shelf and put half a gallon in each of the two five-gallon Jerry cans, then go down to the self-serve fuel pump and fill those cans with Avgas."

Matt sensed the urgency in Michaels' tone.

"You two, pack up the gear, put it on a scale, and get me a weight," Michaels told his friends. "There's a spring scale on the shelf over there. When you're done, meet me in the office, and we'll do a mission brief. We're going to get only one chance to practice this, and we have to discuss weather issues, too."

"All right, Man. Relax," Brian said.

"I'm relaxed, just serious. The flying part is my gig, so I need to plan this out. The rest is up to you two." He stared at them.

"Be right back." Matt left with the gas cans.

"What's with the gas?" Brian tried to change the mood of the conversation.

"Poor man's runway lighting," Michaels said.

"Ah-ha."

The three set to work. Brian and Bob packed the gear, while Michaels hurriedly did the math.

"Hey, what do you guys weigh?" Michaels asked.

"I weigh 240, and Brian weighs 210."

"What about the gear?"

"The scale says fifty-seven, twenty-nine, and seventy. That's

156."

"Is that everything?"

"Nope," Brian said. "The chute weighs thirty-two pounds."

"OK. We have 188, plus you two and me. That makes 838 pounds, plus 360 pounds of fuel. That's 1,198 pounds total. We just make it for this plane."

"What do you mean?" Brian continued rigging his gear. He'd been in a helicopter crash in the Marines, and, while he wasn't afraid to fly in anything, he was skeptical about operating an aircraft near or beyond its limits.

"The useful load on this thing is 1,214 pounds. We're under that by sixteen pounds."

"What happens if we go over?"

"Then the fat guys in the back need to jump out." Keith tried to lighten the mood. "All right. You guys want the good news or the bad news?"

"Bring it on, Dude," Bob said solemnly, loading rounds into the spare clips for the M-4s.

"OK. We have good weather going out tomorrow morning. There's a cold front headed down the state of Florida, and it'll pass through the area sometime tomorrow night, so we'll probably have to fly in some weather on the way home. Any objections to that?"

"Can you and the plane fly in that?" Bob stopped loading and looked at Michaels.

"We have no weather radar in this thing. We'll be flying over water at night. This plane is built like a tank, so it can fly in it, but it might get rough." Weather flying in a single-engine airplane was often terrifying to the uninitiated.

Bob was silent, considering his options. "Dude, if we're on our way back, and no one's shot or dying, I'm fine with it."

"What if someone's been shot?" Brian asked.

"The nearest hospital is on Nassau," Keith said. "You know what, Guys? We'll have to deal with some of these contingencies on the fly. We'll make the call at the time. Agreed?"

The other two nodded.

"All right. For the practice jump, I don't want to risk damaging the gear. Can we fill a duffle with the same weight of something else?"

"Knock yourself out."

"I rigged the chute to allow Bob and me to tandem jump with the gear tethered to us. These are pretty controllable chutes, not like that old military stuff we had. These parafoils are flying wings. You need to drop us one mile upwind for every ten knots of wind. Can you calculate that?"

"Yeah. We have a GPS with an air-data computer in it that's very accurate."

"Perfect."

Matt returned with the gas cans.

"Thanks, Man," Michaels said. "One more thing, then you need to get out of here. Can you take those two duffels and put tools or something in them, so they weigh eighty pounds each?"

"Sure. Do you care what's in 'em, or do you just need the weight?"

"Just the weight."

Matt walked away with the bags.

"Brief me on these NVGs," Keith told Brian.

Bob's Blackberry rang, and he stepped outside to answer. The caller ID read *Em.* Bob knew who it was and why he called. He wasn't in the mood to talk, but he didn't want to exacerbate the situation or compel them to move up the timetable.

"Yes," he said slowly.

"Captain Hershey, I'm very disappointed in you."

"Thank you. That's the nicest thing you've said to me yet."

"Don't you want to save your wife's life? Isn't her safe return important to you?" Hadan taunted Bob, but it didn't work. Bob was a trained hostage negotiator and wouldn't be easily played.

"Let me speak with her. Until I do, we have nothing to discuss." He put the burden back on Hadan.

"That won't happen, Captain Hershey. In a few minutes, you can see her on television. You have a little over twenty-four hours to comply with our demands, or we'll be forced to do what we promised."

"Forced? Who are you kidding?"

"You've been warned, Captain."

"No, you have. You don't know who you're fucking with." He ended the call, knowing that would surprise Hadan.

Hershey played a dangerous game. Taking a deep breath, he forced himself to focus on the job at hand. As he walked into the hangar, the guys loaded the last bag on the plane.

"Everything all right?" Brian knew it wasn't.

"Yeah. That was our towel-headed friend calling to say hi."

"Who?" Matt looked at the others.

"You don't want to know. You got a TV in here, Keith?"

"In the office." He nodded toward the room.

"Let's go." Bob marched toward the office.

"Matt, open the hangar door, pull the plane onto the ramp, close the hangar, and split." Keith placed a hand on Matt's chest to keep him from following Bob.

"All right."

"Matt, don't know too much."

"Yeah. I figured that out already. Can I hold your watch?" That was an old maintenance test pilot and mechanic joke. The mechanic held the pilot's watch when he was on a test flight. If he didn't come back, he could keep it. The point was that most pilots wore expensive watches and would bring back the plane just to reclaim them.

"Sure, Dude." He slipped his Breitling from his wrist and held it out.

"You be careful." Matt slowly accepted the watch.

"I'm always careful. There's no chance I'll die in a small plane."

"It's not the plane I'm concerned about."

"All right. I get it. Now get out of here." Keith walked into the office just in time to catch the end of the broadcast.

Riley was tied to a chair and still wore the same clothes, though there was fresh duct tape across her mouth. She looked tired and worn but otherwise unharmed.

"As for Captain Hershey," Hadan said, glaring into the

camera. "As you can see, your wife is here and is fine for now. Remember what I told you, Captain Hershey." Hadan's expression as he said Bob's name looked like he just tasted shit—an obvious theatrical ploy to provoke Bob. Perhaps it was payback for hanging up on him.

The image switched to a talking head who reviewed the demands Hadan gave and bullet-pointed them on a screen.

Bob grabbed the remote and pushed the *Mute* button.

"What did I miss?" Michaels asked.

"Nothing. The raghead demanded the U.S. stand down its military forces everywhere but in our own country. He wants recognition for Al-Qaeda in the UN, and stuff like that."

Michaels tried to get them to leave the office.

Bob sat on the sofa, staring at the screen, obviously in deep thought. "You know, this doesn't make sense. He's asking me for money and to renounce the government publicly, but he also demands other shit from the government itself."

"I'm no political strategist," Keith said, "but I stayed at a Holiday Inn Express last night, and this looks like a giant stall. It looks like a huge public-relations exercise. They're playing for time."

"What makes you say that?"

"I've spent my life married to an advertising and PR executive. I know a public-relations campaign when I see one. Look what's going on in any country with a Muslim population. These guys are heroes in those places."

"Yeah. How does it end?"

"Think it through to the possible conclusions. What would

happen if they got their asses kicked? What if the powers-that-be caved in to their demands? What happens if they don't, and they execute her? If they let her go with anything less than full compliance of their demands, they look weak. There's no frigging chance the government could stand down the entire U.S. military by tomorrow night, even if the left-wing Looney Tunes in D.C. wanted to. That's why they waited until tonight to make that demand. They know it's impossible. It'll appear that the U.S. didn't comply and give them the justification to go ahead and do the deed. They get to say, 'See? We gave them a chance to save her, but they did nothing.' The same thing happened with Daniel Pearl."

"So what are you saying?"

"I'm saying I think this thing will go down no matter what. We need to be there before eleven PM tomorrow night, and we need to adjust the schedule for that."

The three men looked at each other.

"You know, Bob, he might be right." Brian backed up the less-than-tactfully delivered assessment.

"Let's assume you're right," Bob said. "What do we have to do to get there by ten PM?"

"Here's what I think," Keith said. "We'll do the practice run tonight. Hopefully, that goes as planned, and we learn what we need to know. Tomorrow morning, we launch out of here. It's nearly three hours in that thing to Georgetown.

"We fly over Musha on the way down as low and slow as we can without being obvious. We land at the old Georgetown Airport, ditch the gear, go to the new airport, and clear customs. We get something to eat, fuel the plane, and find a hotel.

"At nine PM, I launch out of there and return to the old airport. There are no lights, so you two will need to mark the end of the runway for me with flares. I won't even shut down. You throw in the gear, and we take off. It'll take thirty minutes to get to altitude over Musha.

"That puts us on the drop zone at 9:45. You'll be on the ground by 9:50. The deal is supposed to go down at 11:00. Sundown is about 5:30, and it's dark by 7:00. We could go earlier than 9:00, but there'll be people up and about, and I don't want to risk being seen. There's a weather front coming in, so we'll have some high overcast. There won't be a moon. What do you think?"

"Sounds good to me," Bob said, "but let's move it up fifteen minutes or half an hour to compensate for the things we don't know we don't know. We can be early, but we can't be late."

"Good with me," Keith said.

"Me, too," Brian acknowledged.

"All right. Let's do this practice run."

They walked out to the small plane. As they climbed in, a twin turboprop taxied past, leaving the smell of burned Jet-A hanging in the air.

"How can you stand that smell?" Bob asked.

"It smells like money to me. I love the smell of Jet-A in the morning."

"All you kerosene cowboys are alike."

"You betcha. And proud of it. I fear the day I can't do this anymore." Michaels fastened his seat belt.

"What do you mean?"

"I'm over fifty. I'm always just one medical exam away from having my license pulled. There are a hundred disqualifying conditions, any one of which ends my career."

"Can that really happen?"

"Yep. Happens all the time."

"Then what?"

"Hell, I don't know. Move to Ohio and become a cop, I guess."

"Not only no, but hell no!"

"Just kidding. I couldn't do that job, anyway."

"Oh, yeah. Hurtling through space in a people-sized mailing tube is much safer."

"Hey, we do what we do."

"Excuse me, Gentlemen," Bob said, interrupting the banter, "but can we leave this love fest for later and get on with the business at hand?" He spoke with his trademarked Thurston Howell the Third yacht-club accent, which was a good sign. It meant he was slipping into cop mode, falling into the routine that kept him alive for twenty-two years on the job.

"Oh, right, Nigel. No time for frivolity," Brian answered in the same high-society voice.

"What's the deal? Are you guys tandem jumping?" Keith asked.

"Yeah," Brian said. "He holds the gear. I hold him, and we all go at once."

"Don't think I'm happy about having a man strapped to my

back, either," Bob added. "Is that a ten mil in your pocket, or are you just happy to see me?"

"No, Man," Brian said. "The ten mil's on my hip. I guess I'm just happy to see you." It wasn't easy, but he managed to make Bob lighten up.

"Better you than me, Dude," Michaels said, before he turned and shouted, "Clear!"

He started the engine. Putting on his headset, he motioned the two men to do the same. "It'll be loud, so wear the headsets, but remember to take 'em off before you jump."

One hour later, they were at 10,000 feet over Airglades Airport. Michaels reduced power to slow the aircraft to jump speed.

"Hey, Guys. The lights at the airport are pilot controlled, and they're off right now. The windsock is lit. See?" Michaels slipped into pilot-in-command mode, pointing out the open door toward the darkened airport below.

"Got it." Brian gave him a thumbs-up.

"All right. I'll make a wide right orbit and put you in position to go. I'll give you ten seconds' warning. Take off your headsets before you depart, please. Anything else you want to tell me?"

"Yeah," Brian said. "Turn off the panel lights before you put on the NVGs, or you'll blind yourself."

"Good point." Keith began his right-hand turn and positioned the NVGs on his head. "After you go, I'll come down at the minimum rate. It'll take me twelve or thirteen minutes. After I land, I'll turn on the runway lights and taxi to the windsock. Sound good?"

"Sounds good to me, Man." Brian wore that infectious grin.

"All right. Ten seconds."

Brian removed his headset, and the two men positioned themselves on the step. Michaels counted down to himself and looked back just as his two comrades disappeared out the door and into the darkness, making the plane lurch precipitously with the weight change.

Keith turned off the panel lights, leaving only the red overhead floodlight to illuminate the instrument panel and flipped down the NVGs. He was surprised at how well he could see, though everything was a monochromatic greenish-white and black.

He closed the throttle all the way, started the timer, and established the aircraft in a minimum sink-rate descent. For the next ten minutes, he needed to learn everything he could about depth perception while using NVGs.

Bob didn't enjoy the canopy deployment. The gear bag was tied to him, and it pulled hard when the chute opened at 5,000 feet, giving Brian time to maneuver. Lower was better, but few people ever looked up. He felt a safe landing was more important and detection was less of a threat.

The chute handled well, and he had no trouble locking onto the drop zone. Over the roar of the wind, he yelled, "Be sure that tether isn't between your legs when we land. It can be left or right but not center."

"Got it!"

"One more thing. Fall forward on landing, not back. Got it?"

"Yeah, Man. Now shut the fuck up and fly this thing."

Brian laughed. Three minutes later, he guided them to a perfect touchdown only thirty feet from the windsock. The gear bag hit the ground first, then Bob, then Brian. They came to rest with Brian under Bob.

"Dude, what part of fall forward didn't you understand? Get off me."

Bob rolled aside. "Now I see why you wanted the tether to one side." He tried to sit upright but couldn't, because he was still strapped to Brian.

Brian pulled the release, and the two men separated. He stood and pulled on the chute, which was tugging on him. "Radio Keith and tell him we're down. I'm gonna grab the chute."

"Will do." Bob pulled a radio from his vest and said, "We're down."

"Got it," Keith replied.

"So much for the test of the tactical communication gear," Bob mumbled.

"So far, so good," Keith said in an empty, dark, quiet airplane. Paying attention to exactly what rate of turn would put him in a position to land without using the engine, he made a mental note of the readings on the cockpit gauges. Airglades was 5,000 feet long, but Rudder Cut wasn't, so he planned to hit the end of the usable runway and stop as short as possible.

"Three thousand feet," he told himself, quickly calculating the turn that led to his final approach. Using the GPS, he created an approach on the screen that showed his final course to the blacked-out runway. All he had to do was align the plane with that course and land using NVGs. The GPS confirmed he was in the right place.

"Two thousand feet, and three miles to go." He peered into the darkness outside through the NVGs, straining to see the runway. "Wow. Holy shit. This thing works."

Still talking to himself, he was amazed at how well he saw the darkened runway and grinned like a kid on Christmas morning.

No longer looking at anything but the runway, he carefully guided the craft to a touchdown. Applying the brakes, he came to a complete stop in less than 600 feet. Idling in the middle of a blacked-out runway was a totally unnatural act for the veteran pilot.

He flipped up the NVGs to marvel at how dark it really was. "Holy shit." That was the most fun he had in an airplane in years. Keying his microphone seven times brought the runway lights up to full brightness and let Bob and Brian see him.

"I never saw you or heard a thing," Bob said into his radio.

"Great. That went better than expected. How'd the jump go?"

"Better than I thought it would, too."

Michaels taxied toward he two men, who jumped into the moving plane before it headed back out to the runway to leave.

Pulling on his headset, Brian said, "That went well."

"Agreed," the other two replied.

They rode home in silence, feeling their adrenalin wear off. Brian made notes. Keith set the autopilot and translated his thoughts into readable form. Bob stared out the open door, facing backward all the way to the airport.

They were as ready as they would ever be. The rest of the tactical issues would have to be addressed in the field. There was no fear, no moment of, "Oh, my God," when one of them realized it was really happening. If anything, the practice jump removed any doubt that the job was doable. Bob achieved emotional separation from the situation, something the other two didn't have to deal with. That ability to turn off emotion was the tactic that kept them alive throughout their professional careers. It was how they ran their lives, and it would enable them to get through their mission.

CHAPTER EIGHT

"Take her back to her room and clean her up. Throw her in the pool, then have her put this on." Hadan handed one of Riley's guards a clean white robe that looked like a burkha without the headdress.

The guard took the robe, and he and his partner grabbed Riley by the armpits and lifted her from the chair. She was exhausted. She hadn't eaten solid food in two days, and all she had to drink was water. She was weak.

"Make sure she gets something to eat," Hadan added. "I need her to be feisty and defiant by tomorrow."

He turned toward the young journalists. "I've made arrangements for us to control the uplink from here tomorrow. Do you understand?" He glared at Mohesh, as much to intimidate him as to gain sadistic pleasure in seeing him squirm when addressed.

"What do you mean, control the uplink from here?" Mohesh didn't understand.

"I mean once we go live tomorrow, they can't turn off the feed. We control the satellite."

"How did you do that?"

"Never mind. It has been done. Once we begin, we must stay on the air until I tell you to kill the feed. You must not lose your nerve, or I'll kill you myself. Do you understand?"

Mohesh nodded.

"Say it."

"Yes...yes, I understand." He had trouble speaking.

"Besides, this lets you both off the hook. You can blame it on me." With a sinister sneer, Hadan turned away.

"What's he doing?" Mohesh asked Padma.

"Don't you get it, you fool? They'll execute that poor woman no matter what. They've already made their decision. The uplink control is to assure them that no one at *Al Jazeera* loses his nerve and blacks them out."

"So why make all the demands? Why three days of transmissions dictating terms? What is this about?"

"It's about power and credibility. It's about playing us and using our network to stage their little execution live and in color on network TV."

"But no one is forcing the other networks to pick up the feed."

"The ratings will force it, as will the Internet. Don't you get it?"

"All I get is if we don't shut up and do what they say, we might be next."

"I'm not sure that isn't a foregone conclusion."

"What?"

"Do you really think they'll let us walk out of here after what we saw and what we have learned?"

"I don't know shit. I'm just a fucking cameraman."

"Great. Well, we have to be on the air in ten minutes. Let's get our shit together and get this segment wrapped up for tonight and try not to think too much about tomorrow."

"I wasn't worried."

"Then you're a bigger fool than I thought." Padma, clearly disgusted, felt legitimate fear for her life. In a few minutes, though, she had to do a live report and try to conceal her concerns from the camera. There was nothing left but to do her job.

As the guards dragged Riley to the Pier House, a Global Hawk circled high above, taking IR video and transmitting the feed to the Langley, Virginia, headquarters of the CIA. Stephen Kirk stood in the situation room, watching it in real time on a giant wall monitor. He saw the two guards with a woman between them traverse the courtyard in front of the Great House and travel the 200 yards down the path to the Pier House before going inside.

The image of the Great House's interior was diffused by the all-metal roofing, but the uplink antenna was visible. The wood roof on the Pier House allowed the camera on the Global Hawk to see inside.

He saw a guard posted at the door, while other guards placed the white, ghost-like image in a room and took positions outside the building's only other obvious entrance. The woman's outline looked as if she lay prone.

"That's good," he told the technician running the console.

The tech reached down and retrieved a jump drive from a computer port and handed it to Kirk, who thanked him and left the room. He went to his office several floors above the situation room.

Plugging the drive into his computer, he made a few keystroke entries before removing the drive and placing it in his pocket.

900 miles away, Bob's Blackberry vibrated in his pocket. Keith was up on a ladder fueling the plane for the next day's departure. Brian sat cross-legged on the hangar floor, repacking the parachute, while Bob inspected weapons and rechecked their gear.

"Guys, take a look at this!"

Keith and Brian, stopping working and peered over his shoulder.

"Can you read the timestamp on that?" Brian asked.

"No. It's too small. Let me at your computer, Keith."

"On the desk. Have at it."

In a few minutes, Bob sent the file to himself and downloaded it from his e-mail.

"Look," Keith noted. "There's no address in the sender box. How do they do that?"

"Who cares? Here it is," Brian said.

"Guys, this is timed zero-five-zero-zero Zulu," Bob said. "That's fifteen minutes ago."

"Let's watch it again," Brian said.

Bob restarted the video.

"Look at that," Brian said. "I guess that answers the question of where she's being kept." He was amazed at the quality of the video feed, far better than anything local law enforcement ever saw. "You know what? I take back every bad thing I ever said about that guy."

"I want to spend some time looking this over, so I can plan some stuff. Why don't you guys finish up and let me do the tactical planning?"

"Good with me." Keith headed for the door.

"I need fifteen minutes to finish with the gear," Brian said, worried Bob might lose focus. "Then we need to get some sleep."

"I'll sleep when I'm dead."

Brian, too tired to argue, went back to the hangar, while Bob stared at the video loop, forming a tactical plan.

Brian met Keith in the hangar. "You good to go, Man?"

"As good as I'm gonna get. Do you really think we can pull this off?"

"Actually, I do. We've got the element of surprise. There's no way they'll be expecting us. They may have intel watching military movement or informants in the government, but no one knows what we're up to."

"Except Kirk."

"Yes, but he basically put his career on the line to give us that intel. There's no way it's a set-up."

"We proved I can do my part. I can get you there and get you out. The rest is up to you two."

"If we do it right, we won't have to fire a single round. No one will get hurt, but I have no problem firing on hostiles."

"Have you thought about what'll happen to your career when we return?"

"If we're successful, we'll be heroes. If not, it probably won't matter."

"Nice thought. Thanks for the pep talk, Coach. I'll go home, have a warm cup of hemlock, and go to bed."

"Hey, I was just saying...."

"No explanation. I get it. Failure isn't an option."

"Correct."

"I'm done. I need to go home and get some sleep. Get Bob, and let's get outta here."

"Yeah. Let's stop for dinner on the way home."

"Are you serious?"

"Yeah. I'm friggin' starving."

"Great."

By nine o'clock the following morning, the three men were climbing into the balmy air. The sun was up in a clear sky. A prefrontal southwest wind gave them a small tailwind on their way to Georgetown.

Leveling off at 9,500 feet, Keith engaged the autopilot and slid the seat all the way back to gain two extra inches of legroom. He pulled a well-worn Thermos from his ragged flight bag and poured a cup of coffee. He flew that route hundreds of times, and each time, he marveled at the sheer beauty of the turquoise-green water below.

The route took them past Isaacs Light. Years earlier, Keith spent days combing the waters off Isaacs, looking for the wreck of a sailboat that belonged to famed restaurateur Chuck Muer. Chuck, along with his wife and another couple, disappeared in a ferocious winter storm. The Coast Guard called off the search without finding so much as a splinter from the boat. The ocean was beautiful but deadly.

They flew over Chub Cay, adjacent to the tongue of the ocean, an oceanographic feature where the edge of the Bahamas shelf dropped off nearly 8,000 feet. The water turned from light green to dark blue in a hard, straight line. From their altitude, it was beautiful. A plane or a ship could disappear in there and never be found.

Once past Nassau, it was time to descend slowly at 500 feet per minute. There was no rush until they reached 1,000 feet above the surface of the blue-green Atlantic. Directly ahead lay Normans Cay on the north end of the Exuma chain. Keith planned to follow the island's southeast boundary, as did every other private pilot flying a single-engine airplane over water.

Down there, there was no traffic-control radar. East of Nassau, there was no Homeland Security. For the next few minutes, it was like flying in 1966, before the tree huggers decided private aviation left an unacceptably large carbon footprint on the environment. Fortunately, no one figured out how to drive to the Bahamas, so flying was still accepted as a necessary form of transportation.

As he flew on, he realized he was probably the last generation to be able to enjoy that. In less than twenty years, such freedom would be gone. It had already vanished in Europe. General aviation never existed in Asia. The only reason it still existed in Africa was the sheer size of the continent and the lack of usable roads, which left no other option.

The airline industry slowly evolved into a government-owned, government-run public utility that, like the post office, didn't make money. Salaries dropped to the point that the industry no longer attracted the best and brightest, and even those who would do it for free, for the sheer love of it, found no joy in the endless government regulations and red tape. Kids were no longer intrigued by the allure of flight.

Keith's son had no interest in flying, even though he flew as a passenger with him since he was six months old. The image of the dashing pilot was dead. Insurance issues had all but killed air racing. Heroes, like Roscoe Turner and Jimmy Doolittle, whose names were household words in the twenties and thirties because of air racing, were unknown to modern youth. Commercial airline pilots had been reduced to bus drivers in the sky.

Keith sat quietly, waxing nostalgic for the time when he took the number-seven train to Astoria, then walked seventeen blocks to the Flushing Airport, the nearest general-aviation airport to his house. He washed planes all day for the chance to take one hop around the patch. Those good times were long gone.

Closing his eyes, he sipped his coffee, a simple pleasure he still allowed himself. The smell and taste took him to another place and time, the same way that hearing an old song could bring back a specific time and place. He did that all his life. He belonged in the sky.

He glanced back at Brian, who slept in the back seat, then tapped Bob's leg and motioned him to look at their unconscious friend. Bob smiled and shrugged.

As they passed over Normans Cay, Keith carefully positioned the aircraft to the east side of the chain of islands, so Brian and Bob could get a good look at Musha as they passed.

"Hey, Guys. Musha in five minutes."

Brian instantly opened his eyes as if they never closed. He and Bob took cameras from their bags and tested them.

"I'll slow down a little," Keith said, "but I can't go too slow, because it would look obvious from the ground."

"Can you give me just a little bank as we go over," Bob asked, "so I can shoot straight down?"

"Sure thing."

Cindy Fink ran across the courtyard in front of the Great house. She looked out of place on a tropical island wearing white short-shorts and three-inch open-toed heels. Even at her age, she had spectacular legs, and she never missed a chance to show them off. Her flowered blouse was tied at the waist to show off her fit abs, and it was tactfully unbuttoned to show what she believed was just enough cleavage.

"Charles! Charles!" she shouted.

Caretaker turned to answer her. Everyone in the Bahamas called him Caretaker, but Fink always used his given name.

"Charles, how are you this morning?" Without waiting for an answer, she continued, "Our guests will be checking out tomorrow, but I have a special request for food this evening."

She rummaged through her clipboard and produced a grocery list. "The kitchen asked that you pick up these things on today's supply run to Georgetown. Can you do that for me, please?"

Caretaker took the list without looking at it and placed it in his shirt pocket. "Certainly, Ma'am. I'll attend to it personally."

"Ma'am! How many times have I asked you not to call me that? It makes me feel old."

"My apologies, er, Ms. Fink. I'll attend to it." He didn't care much for her but was far too good at hiding his true feelings to ever let her sense his dislike.

As they spoke, a maid walked across the courtyard carrying a food tray.

"Excuse me, Ms. Fink." He held up his index finger and addressed the maid. "Where are you off to, my dear?" He smiled.

"This is for the woman in the Pier House."

"Wait. I'm going that way, anyway. Allow me to take that for you."

She gladly handed him the tray. All three of them glanced up at the small plane flying overhead, but that happened constantly.

"If you'll excuse me, Ms. Fink, I'll deliver this and head over to Georgetown," Caretaker said. "I need to get to the post office, too, so I'll return around three this afternoon."

"Very well. See you later."

"Good day, Ms. Fink."

Caretaker walked down the path to the Pier House, the most-recently built house on the island. Copperfield built it during his short tenure as owner of the island at a cost of more than one million dollars. Small and secluded, it had a magnificent view of the ocean. The tiny cove, created by a small spit of land that hooked around in a U, protected the shore from the beating surf.

As he approached the house, a guard rose from his chair. Without speaking, he opened the door and walked in, as Caretaker followed. They went to the bedroom, where Riley had been tied to the bed and blindfolded.

"Put the tray over there." The guard pointed to a small table between the bed and double-wide French doors looking down the pier, while he released Riley's restraints. As she sat up on the bed, she pulled off the blindfold, but the room's brightness made her squint.

"You can go, Old Man," the guard said.

"If you don't mind, kind sir, I'll wait to bring back the tray, so I don't have to return later."

"Very well. Stand over there, but don't get in the way."

"As you wish, Sir." Caretaker moved to the corner.

"You must eat," the guard commanded Riley.

Without warning, he lifted her by the armpits. In one brisk, violent move, he propelled her from the bed to the chair beside the table. Riley was too weak and hungry to fight.

The guard untied her wrists and stepped back. She opened her eyes and saw food in front of her. She quickly ate the toast, eggs, and sliced fruit. She chugged down the orange juice like a high-school girl at a keg party. Not all of it went into her mouth, but she didn't care.

She became aware that Caretaker stood in the corner near

the door, but she didn't know who he was. It was the first time she was in the room without wearing a blindfold, and she wanted more time to look around.

"I've been tied to the bed for two days," she said to the guard. "May I stand up and stretch before I drink this tea?" She looked at him with puppy-dog blue eyes.

The guard thought for a moment. "Make it quick."

Riley stood and stepped around the chair, scanning the room, as she turned. She placed her elbows on the chair and straightened her legs, deliberately showing her ass to the guard, who didn't mind looking. Rolling her head from side-to-side, she appeared to be stretching her neck but was again scanning the room.

Standing upright, she placed her wrists behind her back, forcing her chest forward while the guard watched. As she looked around the room, she made mental notes of everything—windows, doors, air vents—anything that might be useful if she were lucky enough to escape her restraints.

Squatting down, she extended one leg toward the French doors, then reached for her foot with both hands, allowing her a quick look outside. To continue the charade, she extended the other foot in the opposite direction, toward the door where Caretaker stood.

Then she stood and smiled at the guard. "Thanks. I'll take that tea now."

The guard removed the teapot from the tray and motioned to Caretaker. "Here. Take this back to the kitchen. Leave the teapot and cup."

Caretaker walked to the table, his eyes locked on Riley. "Will there be anything else, Ma'am?"

"Don't speak to her!" the guard warned. "Take the tray and go."

"No, thank you." She looked Caretaker in the eye.

"As you wish." He avoided eye contact with the guard, as he picked up the tray and left.

"Finish your tea," the guard said. "Then it's back in the bed."

"I understand. Is there some chance you can tie me in a different position? I've been in the same position for two days."

"No. Now finish."

"OK, OK." She poured tea into the china cup and sipped for a few minutes.

Finally, the guard became impatient. "Back in the bed."

"OK, but can I use the bathroom first?"

"No!" He grabbed her arm.

"Please! I'll be quick."

"I can't let you out of my sight."

"Really? You can watch if you want."

The guard was unprepared for a Western woman, much less Riley, and decided to call her bluff.

"OK." He released her arm and pointed to the bathroom a few steps away. The toilet was visible from where he stood. "Don't close the door."

"Deal." She walked into the lavatory and did her business in full view of the guard, who couldn't believe it. In his country, a woman would never speak to a man without permission, much less behave like that. Riley took the opportunity to look around some more.

She stood from the toilet and washed her hands and face, knowing the watchful guard studied her from the corner of his eye. She didn't know what she would do, but at least she knew where she would do it."

"OK. I'm ready." She walked toward the bed while drying her hands and face with a towel with the letters *MC* monogrammed on it. Tossing the towel on the bed, she noticed the robe Hadan gave the guard the previous night. She hadn't seen it earlier. "Is that for me?"

"For later. Not now!" The guard scowled.

Riley piled up pillows into an upright position and climbed into the bed, putting her hands over her head. "Can you tie me like this, please?"

The guard didn't know what to make of her. Picking up the rope, he tied her hands together, then to the headboard.

"Thank you."

He moved to replace the blindfold.

"Please, no!"

He wasn't listening. She was blindfolded, her hands tied to the headboard, and one foot tied to one of the massive posts of the four-poster bed. At least she wasn't gagged.

Her surroundings were elegant. The furniture was expensive, as were the wall treatments, window dressings, and rugs. It was obvious she wasn't being held on an uninhabited rock. She didn't know how to escape the room. Even if she managed that, where would she go? Where the hell was MC? Was it a place or the owner's initials? She had no way to know.

The guard returned to his seat in front of the door. Riley tested the bindings on her wrists and ankles. She didn't have anything else to do.

CHAPTER NINE

Debbie tried to stick to her usual routine. After returning home from the gym, she went into her home office to answer her e-mail and pay bills. She tried to use the routine to keep her mind off what she knew was going to happen.

On top of Keith's computer, she saw the letter addressed to her son and couldn't resist reading it. As she read the words, she heard Keith's voice in her mind.

> *Matthew,*
>
> *If you're reading this, it's because things didn't go well. I don't know what the news will say or what you'll be told, but I need you to know some things. What I did here, I did not out of misguided loyalty or friendship, but because I believed it was the right thing. I need you to know that and to remember me as the guy who ran into the fire when everyone else ran away.*

He referred to an incident when Matthew was only seven years old. They would hang out at the airport on a Sunday morning, just father and son. Together they would sit on a golf cart, ride around, and watched airplanes take off and land. It was their quality time.

One Sunday, a large-piston twin lost control and crashed in the middle of the field less than one hundred yards from them. Keith handed his son his cell phone, told him to call 911, and then ran toward the plane.

The aircraft split open on impact, and one wing burned. Two passengers crawled from the wreckage and ran away, even though another was trapped inside, screaming.

Keith ran past the two stunned passengers and crawled into the plane, dragging the last victim from the wreckage while still strapped to her seat.

As they emerged from the smoldering hulk, the fuel tank ignited. The explosion knocked Keith to the ground. He regained his footing and continued dragging the woman, still in the seat, away from the burning plane.

Matthew sat in the golf cart, watching the entire event unfold after he dialed 911.

Minutes later, paramedics and a fire-rescue team arrived, along with local news media. Keith refused medical treatment and all interviews, speaking only to law enforcement. The pilot died in the crash.

Keith didn't perceive his actions as heroic. It was simply the right thing to do. When they went home that afternoon, Matthew told his mommy, "Daddy ran into the fire while everyone else ran away."

*I know you'll be OK in life. I've
known that since you were ten, on
the night you won the state
championships. I was so proud of
you. I always have been. I haven't
done anything great with my life. I
didn't find a cure for cancer, walk
on the moon, or set an unbreakable
speed record, but I did raise you.
You're about all the proof on earth
that I ever existed.
I hope I taught you to follow your
heart, to do what you love. When
and if the time comes that you must
do something simply because it's
the right thing, I hope you have the
strength and wisdom to do it.
With any luck, you won't have to
read this. If not, always remember I
love you. Dad.*

Tears welled in Debbie's eyes. The realization that Keith felt it necessary to leave the note for Matthew told her that whatever they were planning, it was more dangerous than he led her to believe.

She picked up the phone and called Keith, but the connection went directly to voicemail. She hung up without leaving a message.

As they passed over Musha, the men took pictures. Keith banked the high-winged Maule gently to the right to afford an almost-unobstructed view of the ground to his comrades.

Bob shot stills, while Brian took video. With only one pass, they shot as fast as they could. Fifteen seconds later, they passed over Musha and flew over Rudder Cut, taking pictures of the runway, the docks, and the water between the islands.

A few moments later, it was all behind them.

"Hope you guys got what you needed," Keith said.

"Me, too," Brian said over the intercom.

"All right. Let's go ditch the gear."

Twenty minutes later, they touched down at the old Georgetown airport. The runway was in horrible condition. Weeds two-feet-tall grew through cracks in the crumbling concrete, and Keith didn't want to whack them with the propeller. He guided the plane to where the foundation of the old terminal building stood. Beside it was the containment wall for the old fuel farm, though the tanks were gone.

"I say we ditch the gear in the corner of the containment basin and cover it with loose trash, like those skids." Keith pointed out the window, as the plane shuddered to a stop. "Come on. We need to get it done before we're seen."

Hopping out of the plane, Keith walked quickly to the other side of the aircraft and opened the cargo doors. Brian sat just inside with the gear. Bob left the plane and scouted a place to hide their gear.

"Over here!" Bob called.

The three men quickly stashed and covered the bags, then jumped back into the plane. Keith started the engine, turned into the wind, and took off from the middle of the tarmac. Without the gear and already light on fuel, the machine leapt into the air in a few hundred feet.

"Wow!" Bob said.

"Like that?" Keith grinned at him.

"Yeah, Man. Not bad for a little puddle jumper."

"Nope. Not bad at all."

Minutes later, they landed at the big airport, officially known as Exuma International.

As they taxied in, Keith tapped Bob. "There's Musha's Twin Otter."

"How do you know it's theirs?" Brian asked.

"I used to fly it when Melk owned it. N622JM."

As they approached close enough to read the tail number, it was what Keith said. He taxied to the ramp of the only FBO on the airport and shut down. As they climbed out, a big black lineman walked over from the terminal building. He stood over six-feet tall and weighed 250 pounds.

"Hey, Man," Keith said in greeting.

"Good mornin'. How long you staying with us?"

"A couple of days at least. Does Junior still work here?"

"Junior the boss now. He own it, Mon."

"Really? Good for him. I've known him a long time, but I haven't seen him in years."

"I'm his son, Kenny." He extended his hand.

"Little Kenny?"

"Not so little anymore." He laughed and tapped his stomach, acknowledging his size.

"I remember you. I used to fly that Otter over there with Captain Chuck. Do you remember him?"

"Oh, sure, Mon. How he doin'?"

"He's retired a long time now. He lives in Tennessee and quit flyin'."

"Well, you tell him Little Kenny say hi for me."

"I'll do that. Can I get you to top this thing off with one hundred low lead for me?"

"Sure ting."

"Is Customs still in the same place?"

"This dah Bahamas, Mon. No-ting change in dah Bahamas."

"Good. I'll be back to pay for that fuel after we clear Customs."

"OK, Mon. See you."

Keith walked to his comrades, who pretended to be busy and stayed out of the conversation.

"You know him?" Bob asked.

"Yeah. His dad owns the place. The last time I saw him, he was maybe twelve-years old. He remembers my ex-partner. It's all good. Let's go clear Customs. After that, I gotta come back to pay for the fuel. Then we can walk across the street to the Conch Inn and get some lunch."

"You know the restaurants here, too?"

"Dude, you're in for a treat. This place is for locals, not tourists. It has the best conch chowder on earth."

"I'm game," Brian said.

"There's a surprise," Bob said. "How the fuck do you eat so much and stay so skinny?"

"Easy. No doughnuts."

"Funny. No doughnut jokes, please."

The two men were in full law-enforcement mode. Keith might as well have been invisible, but he let them go on. It was a good way to relieve tension.

The Conch Inn looked like it was right out of a movie set— dark, musty, and the lighting sucked. It was the closest thing to a sports bar on the island, and it predated the airport. The walls were covered with photos and newspaper clippings of locals who did anything newsworthy, though the Bahamian definition of newsworthy wasn't the same as in the States.

It was a local place, so the articles showed people catching a big fish, delivering a baby, or winning a scholarship to school. It was a small town on steroids. Tourists were encouraged to dine elsewhere. Pilots and fishermen, however, were welcome.

Keith spent many afternoons at the Conch Inn, when he flew charter. Back then, dressed in full uniform, he had a viable excuse to refuse to drink Kalik, the local beer. He wasn't much of a beer drinker, anyway, but Kalik was just plain awful. The three wore bush shorts, fishing shirts, and baseball caps. They looked as if they just got off a boat after a long morning of bone fishing.

Pulling up a table in the middle of the room, the men scanned their surroundings for different things. Keith, feeling slightly nostalgic, wanted to see what had changed since his last visit. Bob and Brian checked the local crowd like cops, noting the exits and the TV on the bar. It was unusual to see a cathode-ray TV in the States anymore, but in the Bahamas, they were common. Thankfully, it was tuned to a soccer match, not the news.

Keith ordered conch fritters and conch chowder and a round of Kalik. Conversation was light, and the food was good. Brian had his back to the door, while Bob faced the entrance. Brian watched an old man sitting in the corner by the restroom doors. After a moment, Brian stood and excused himself.

"Don't catch anything while you're in there," Bob said, as Brian walked toward the back.

He returned a few minutes later.

"Everything come out OK?" Bob teased.

"I'm fine, Dude, but that old guy in the corner has been eye-fucking you since we walked in."

"How do you know it's me?"

"I walked past him twice, and he didn't take his eyes off you."

Bob, who had his back to the old man, wasn't about to turn around.

"In a minute, I'm gonna get up and go to the head. Let's see what he does." He finished his beer and set down the bottle. "If he follows me in, trust me, I'll be waiting. Give me thirty seconds before you come save him."

Bob stood and walked toward the bathroom.

"Is he kidding?" Keith asked.

"I don't think so," Brian replied. "Let's see what happens."

Bob walked past the old man and went into the crumbling restroom, letting the door shut behind him.

The moment the door closed, the old man slid from his booth to follow Bob.

"There he goes," Brian said.

"How'd you spot him?" Keith wondered.

"He was obvious. He locked on us when we walked in and never took his eyes off Bob. When I went to the head, the old guy continued staring at our table, so I knew it wasn't me." He remembered Keith hadn't worked in law enforcement. "It's a cop thing."

"Great, Kojak. Are you going after him?"

"Bob said thirty seconds. I'll wait."

The old man opened the door and entered the restroom. Bob, waiting behind the door, shoved it closed, spun the old man around, and pinned him against the wall with his hands on his throat. "Who are you, and why are you following me?"

Caretaker desperately tried to squeak out a reply, but Bob's hands were so large, they completely surrounded his neck, making breathing, much less talking, almost impossible. "I...I know...."

Bob loosened his grip slightly. "You know what?"

The old man coughed. "I know who you are and why you're here." He spoke in a whisper.

"How do you know? Are you one of them?"

"Please, Sir, let me down, and I'll tell you."

Bob paused and decided the old man wasn't an immediate threat, so he released his grip. "Start talking."

"I'm Charles Hardon Holly the second." He saluted like a British Army officer, his palm toward Bob.

Brian and Keith walked in. Bob and the old man stopped and looked at them.

"Are we interrupting something?" Brian asked.

"Close the door, Keith, and stay on it," Bob ordered.

Keith braced his back against the closed door.

"Gentlemen," Brian said, "meet Charles Hardin Holly the second. He says he know who we are and why we're here."

"Really?" Brian asked.

"No," Caretaker said. "I said I know who *you* are and why *you're* here." He nodded at Bob.

"Yeah? How do you know that?"

"I watch the news. I happen to be the caretaker at Musha Cay. I saw you walk into the bar. It didn't take much to put two and two together."

"You work at Musha?" Bob asked, excited. "You've seen her?"

"I saw her this morning. In fact, I brought her breakfast."

"She's OK?"

"As of this morning, yes."

"How many of them are there? Where are they, and...."

"Wait a minute." Brian grabbed Bob's shoulder, pulling him

away from the man. "How do you know you can trust anything he says?"

Caretaker anticipated the question. "I knew her father."

"Oh?" Bob asked. "How's that?"

Caretaker took a deep breath. "I was the pilot of the plane he was on when he disappeared."

"Shit, Bob," Brian said in disgust. "He could've read that on the friggin' Internet."

"Yeah, that's true. Tell me, Charles Hardin Holly the second, what kind of plane was it?"

"A Piper Aztec."

"What was her father's name?"

"William Forsythe Smith, but everyone called him Smitty."

"What's Riley's real name?"

"Emily Riley Smith." He didn't hesitate or flinch with his answers.

"How did you survive the crash and he didn't?"

"I don't know. We had a mechanical problem at night and went into the ocean. When I woke up, I was on a Coast Guard cutter. They never found Smitty."

"Well, that's friggin' convenient," Brian said.

"No, no," Keith said. "Let him talk."

"They're keeping her in a house near the Great House, called the Pier House. They take her to the Great House every night around ten."

"Tell me about the guards," Bob said.

"There are two guards all the time. Eight total. They work in pairs, in shifts. There are two older gentlemen who wear white robes most of the time. I'm sure they're the bosses. There are two young kids who came on the boat with your wife, and two reporters, but they aren't armed, and I almost never see them leave the Great House. They told us we need to be in our rooms every evening by nine and not to come out for any reason. That has been the routine for the last three nights."

"All right, Charles Hardin Holly the second, do you want to help?"

"Of course."

"Then go about your business as if we never had this conversation. Tell no one you saw us."

"That's it? Oh, I see. You think I'm nothing but an old man. That I'll just get in the way. Let me tell you, Sir, I served in the Royal Marines!"

He pulled back his collar to reveal the unit insignia of the Royal Marines tattooed on his chest, pushing out his rib cage so Bob could see better.

"No, Sir, that's not it at all. Just let us do what we came to do."

Clearly insulted, Caretaker took a moment to tuck in his shirt and dust himself off. "Very well, then. I should be on my way."

"Yes, you should." Bob sounded patronizing, condescending, and sarcastic.

Caretaker stumbled past Bob and Brian, never taking his eyes off Bob. Keith still blocked the door.

"It's all right," Bob said. "Let him go."

Keith stepped back. Caretaker reached for the doorknob, then turned back toward Bob.

"Good luck."

"Thanks."

He left, closing the door behind him.

"What the fuck?" Keith asked.

"What did you want me to do, kill him right here in the bathroom? He can't do us any good."

"How do you know he won't run right back there and tip them off?"

"Because he told the truth."

"How can you tell?"

"Because nowhere was it ever reported what kind of aircraft Riley's father was flying or that his nickname was Smitty. I know that only because Riley told me. Only someone with firsthand knowledge would know that."

"That's it? That's all you're going on?"

"Yeah, and that he gave up what we already knew. They're keeping her in that house with the dock on it, but he didn't know we knew. He could have told us anything, so yeah, that's it."

"Wow."

"Wow what?"

"It seems a little too convenient."

"It is what it is. Let's go."

Bob, pushed past the other two, went out the door, as Keith looked at Brian for a reaction.

"It's his party," Brian said. "He can choose the music." He

followed Bob out.

"Great." Keith went out next.

They took rooms at the Peace and Plenty Resort, in the middle of town. It was past three o'clock in the afternoon. Brian and Bob wanted to review the photos and video they took and plan the tactical details. Keith wanted to sleep, which was his way of dealing with stress.

"I'm going to nod off for a while," Keith said. "Wake me around six.

"You got it, Man," Bob said.

Keith briefly toyed with the idea of calling Debbie, but he didn't want to implicate her if the mission went badly, so he showered, pulled the drapes, and crawled into bed to sleep.

Two hours later, Keith sat bolt upright when he heard someone pound on his door.

"Wake up, Sleepy Head!" a voice called, as if waking a two-year-old from a nap. It took Keith a moment to remember where he was.

"Coming!" He had a pasty dry mouth, a byproduct of the ancient window air conditioner and his tendency to breathe through his mouth when he slept.

Opening the door, he squinted at the bright light. "What up, Po Po?" He shielded his eyes from the glare.

"Look at that," Brian said. "The old white guy speaks ghetto."

"I just wanted you two five-oh types to feel at home when

you knock on the door of a cheap motel."

"Five-oh types? You've been watching reruns of *Cops*. Funny, but when you went to bed, I could swear you were an old white guy. When you woke up, you be a gang bang-ah, a real play-ah." Brian made a gang sign with his hands, pulling them in front of his chest and extending the pinky and thumb.

"Yeah, that's me, Notorious O.L.D. Come in, but give me a minute to get my shit together."

"You need help with that, too, or did you take your fiber and Geritol?"

"Naw. Bob said you two finished the Geritol."

"You two are having way too much fun," Bob said.

"I may be old, but you ugly," Keith said.

"Get your old ass together, so we can get outta here. We got things to do and asses to kick."

There was no tension, fear, or anxiety as the men joked, which was their defense mechanism. Keith stuffed his flight suit into his backpack. Everything else was with their gear. "I'm ready. What are we doing?"

"I got us a scooter. I'll run you down to the airport, come back, get Brian, and head for the Georgetown Airport. We'll meet you there at nine sharp."

"OK. Take three of the emergency flares from the plane and mark the runway. Put two on the approach end and one at the departure end. I'll cycle the landing lights on and off once when I'm three miles out on final. That will give you ninety seconds to light the flares and meet me at the gear. I don't want to shut down. I'll take the pins out of the cargo door before takeoff. Take the door off the plane and leave it behind. We don't have the room for it. Got that?"

"Got it," Bob replied.

"One more thing."

"What's that?"

"In case this thing goes south...."

"Dude, don't even say it."

Keith looked at them.

"All right."

Taking a deep breath, he checked his watch. I've got nineteen twenty-two and thirty seconds in ten, nine, eight, seven, six, five, four, three, two, one."

The three men synchronized their watches.

Walking outside into the cool evening air, Keith noticed the stiff southwest wind, a sure sign a cold front was approaching. He'd been out of touch with a computer or TV all day and hadn't seen a weather report since before departing that morning. Fortunately, the aircraft was equipped with a satellite weather receiver that was as good as anything he could learn from a computer. They were ahead of schedule, so he could spend a few minutes giving himself a good weather briefing.

Keith climbed onto the scooter behind Bob. "Guess you're getting used to having a guy strapped to your back, eh Big Boy?"

"Oh, stop!" Bob said in a feminine voice. Changing to his normal tone, he said, "Hang on tight."

As they whizzed through the streets of Georgetown, Keith noticed the place had a rustic charm that hadn't changed since the sixties. Brightly painted houses and shops, with neatly manicured grounds, contrasted with abysmal roads and total lack of street lighting or traffic signage.

It was a short ride to the airport. A little before eight, Bob stopped the scooter in front of an unsecured gate. A cat dug through a trash can in front of the airport cantina, the only living thing in sight.

"Come out to the plane to take those flares," Keith said.

"Yep."

They walked to the parked aircraft. Keith opened the cargo door and rummaged through his survival bag, emerging with six flares and handing them to Bob.

"All right, Dude. See you over at Georgetown."

"You got it." Keith turned to prep the plane.

"Listen." Bob held his arm. "I can't tell you how much this means to me."

"Forget it. You know what? If you went and did this without me, or never even asked, I'd have been pissed."

Bob smiled. "I understand."

"Now get going, and be careful."

Bob gave him a quizzical look. That was a strange comment considering what they planned.

"That scooter is a death trap," Keith explained. "You drive like a maniac."

Bob laughed and walked away.

Keith checked the oil, deciding to add a quart, since there wouldn't be time later. Both fuel tanks were full. He carefully pulled the cotter pins from the hinges that held the cargo door to the aircraft and tossed them. All they had to do was open the doors and push out the clevis pins to remove the door.

He untied the aircraft and pulled the chock from the tail wheel. Taking the pistol from the flare kit, he loaded a twelve-gauge star shell into the chamber and placed the gun in the pocket on the pilot's door. His watch read 8:30 PM.

The plane was ready. He climbed in and started the battery-powered auxiliary GPS system. It soon locked onto the satellite constellation and downloaded current weather info. While that ran, he carefully reviewed his notes from the practice run the previous night.

After a few minutes, the GPS downloaded current radar and satellite cloud images, displaying them on the screen. Wind was from 160 degrees at fifteen knots, gusting to twenty. It was nearly a direct crosswind at Rudder Cut, but he could handle it. Cloud tops were high, at more than 20,000 feet, so they would block the moon without affecting their flight.

A line of thunderstorms moved off the South Florida coast toward the Gulf Stream. They'd have to negotiate that on the way home, if they got that far.

"I'll deal with that later," he muttered.

Keith stopped in midthought. He sat in a silent, blacked-out aircraft, about to break a dozen laws in two different countries, and he was totally calm. "Wow. Here we go."

He flipped the master switch, and the electric gyro spooled up to speed. Reaching down, he pushed the mixture control to the full rich position while turning the starter key with his free hand. The little Maule started on the first blade. He carefully turned up the cockpit lights to a very dim setting, to preserve his night vision. There were no runway or taxi lights, but he didn't need them. The plane was so light; it wouldn't remain on the ground for long.

He waited a minute for the oil temperature to rise, noted the time, and wrote it at the top of his flight log as *8:51*. Not willing to do an engine run-up for fear of someone hearing him, he decided to take off from his parking spot. Holding the brakes, he ran the throttle up to full power, checked the gauges one last time, and released the brakes.

The lightly loaded plane leaped forward and was in the air almost instantly. Keith deliberately left the external lights off on the off chance that, if someone heard him depart, they wouldn't see which way he flew.

Keith climbed into the night sky. At 1,000 feet, he leveled off and reduced power. The air was smooth, and the island below was visible in the ambient light. The ship's GPS gave him an instant distance and bearing.

He was only four miles from the pickup. He lined up with the runway heading of 110 degrees and flashed his landing lights. A moment later, he saw one, then two flares, followed by a third a few seconds later farther in the distance. He slowed the plane to sixty-five knots.

As he neared the touchdown zone, he realized he couldn't see the ground well enough to know when to flare. He decided to turn on his landing lights at fifty feet, just long enough to allow a smooth touchdown. He passed the two flares and turned on his lights. In the soft glow of the landing light, directly in the middle of the runway, he saw four fifty-five-gallon drums painted bright yellow.

"What the...?" He lifted the nose to float over them and land beyond. "Shit!" His heart pounded.

How had those drums appeared since that morning? Who did it? Keith rolled to the end of the runway where the gear was stashed. He turned the aircraft and shut down. Bob and Brian, already dressed, carried the gear toward the plane.

"I thought you didn't want to shut down," Brian said.

"I wasn't planning on it, but did either of you see the fifty-five-gallon drums in the middle of the runway?"

"No. I rode the scooter down the side and lit the flares, but I didn't see any barrels."

"They're out there. Someone must've seen us land this morning and told the authorities. This airport is closed."

"There's nothing we can do about it now," Bob said. "Can we still take off?"

"Yeah, no problem, as soon as I get this seat cushion out of my ass. Load the gear." Those barrels ruined Keith's peace. He waited for the adrenalin to wear off, but it wasn't likely to happen soon.

"Ready, Dude?" Bob asked.

Keith, looking over his shoulder, saw Bob and Brian in the plane, attaching their harness.

"Here's your bag, Man." Brian handed him a large black backpack.

Keith strapped it to the copilot's seat. As he reached for the key, he caught a whiff of the familiar scent of Tiger Balm.

"Which one of you two is wearing Tiger Balm for aftershave?"

"I am!" they replied simultaneously.

"Ah-ha! Who's the old guy now?" He wore a satisfied grin, as he started the engine and took off.

CHAPTER TEN

"Not as good as back home, but acceptable," KSM commented on the quality of the couscous.

"I'm glad you're pleased," Hadan said.

"Is everything ready for tonight?"

"Yes. We have control of the satellite and can't be cut off. All the major western networks have agreed to carry the feed, except one. Our friends at *Al Jazeera* will make a small fortune on this tonight."

"Ah, the decadent West. So predictable. They'd do nothing to stop us, but they'll pay money to watch it."

"It's better than I hoped. All around the globe, Muslims are turning out to support us. They sense this is a critical moment. We have their undivided attention."

Throughout the US, anti-American Muslim groups gathered at execution parties as if it were a sporting event. The White House kept a low profile. Officially, the administration refused to acknowledge that Riley's abduction ever happened, much less on American soil, yet the daily White House press briefing was filled with warnings for the general public. They weren't told about impending danger but were asked not to seek retribution on those who partook of such activities. The White House took great pains to emphasize that everyone had a constitutional right to freedom of expression and cited the Nazi march in Skokie, Illinois, as a precedent.

In 1977, the Nazis, assisted by the ACLU, won the right to march in Skokie, a predominantly Jewish community. That was a low point in the distortion of constitutional law and was considered a key factor in the next election, which was won by Ronald Reagan, a conservative. The press briefing left out those details, of course, though it mentioned *swift and immediate* legal action against anyone who acted against the participants of such activities.

"Yes, we do. It must go smoothly, as well as with Daniel Pearl." They spoke as if discussing a dinner party, not an execution.

"It will. I'm going to my room to prepare myself. I'll meet you at the Great House at ten-thirty."

"Excellent. We go on the air at ten forty-five. I've prepared the speech, as you instructed. Do you wish to see it?" Hadan asked.

"That won't be necessary. I'm sure you'll do as I asked." KSM stood, his two bodyguards emerging from the shadows like ghosts. "We're on the cusp of a great shift in global power, Hadan." He paused, then turned back. "Ten-thirty?"

"Yes."

KSM walked off with his two bodyguards following.

Hadan looked west across the water into the night, struggling to find a single fiber in him that cared about the glory of God, the global shift of power, and the rise of the Muslim faith. He realized he didn't give a rat's ass about any of it. For him, it was about hate, revenge, and retribution. He hated the West for what he believed was the oppression of his people. He sought revenge against those whom he was taught were his mortal enemies. He wanted retribution on those who imprisoned him.

Four years in an American university were no match for thousands of years of twisted tradition that had been hijacked and perverted by a few powerful men. They managed to steal an entire religion and create other men like Hadan, who knew nothing but hatred of those he was taught to hate. It took generations to reach that point, the work of his father and his father's father.

It was his moment, his time. He felt no remorse for what was about to happen and didn't see any moral depravity in his plans. For Hadan and thousands like him, that was how it had to be done. He knew around the world, those who thought like him and believed that was the proper way, would follow in his footsteps. Many people would be executed that night. The fact that it happened globally and in unison would shake the very foundations of the society he hated.

He would finally affect the change his father and his father's father worked for. It was vindication, proving that the ends justified the means. That much he knew.

KSM would get the glory. With Al-Zawahiri dead, Hadan was right behind him in the lineup of future leadership. No one alive knew Hadan gave up Al-Zawahiri for the twenty-five-million-dollar reward money. No one left alive knew he cut a deal with the Americans through the Pakistani government. He covered his tracks too well. It was easy. All he had to do was provide the time and place, and the

U.S. cruise missiles did the rest. The money, transferred to a Swiss bank account, was routed through Pakistan, then a Damascus bank, making it untraceable.

Since Hadan handled Al-Qaeda's finances, he knew no one would even look for him. Twenty-five million would buy a lot of friends if things went bad. Hadan didn't give a shit about the glory of Allah. All he cared about was himself. It was survival of the fittest. He would do what he must and say what he must to get what he wanted.

He was very good at that. The evening's events, if they went as planned, would propel his career to new heights. His name would become synonymous with those of KSM and UBL. It was coming together as he dreamed it would.

Hadan turned toward the Great House and started walking. After a few steps, his guards emerged from the shadows.

Hadan motioned to one. "Find Rushi and Akshay and tell them to be in the Great house at ten-thirty. Tell them it's an honor to share in the vengeance of their fathers. Once that's done, check the guards and make sure all the island staff are secure for the night. I don't want any surprises. Understand?"

The guard nodded without speaking, then ran off in double-time.

Two miles up in the air and two miles south, the trio prepared for their jump run.

"Right on time, Guys," Keith said over the intercom. "Are you ready?"

"Ready as we're gonna be," Brian said.

"Yeah, I'm ready," Bob snorted.

"OK. I'll make a right-hand circle into the drop zone. I'll give you a ten-second countdown just like our practice. The rest is up to you."

"What's the GPS say the wind is up here?" Brian asked loudly over the roar of the open cargo door.

"One eight zero at sixteen at this altitude. It's closer to ten at the surface."

"Got it. Ready, Dude?" Brian tapped Bob's shoulder, as the two men faced the open door.

"Good to go," Bob said.

Keith reduced power and slowed the aircraft to sixty-five knots, down from their cruising speed of over 100. The cabin quieted, as the two men in the rear removed their headsets and positioned themselves at the door, Bob on the step, with Brian sitting in the door, his legs dangling in the slipstream.

Keith carefully lined up for the jump. No one spoke. Each man concentrated on the task at hand. Conditions were better than expected, and the island lights made details visible even from their altitude.

"I'm not gonna pull the chute until three thousand feet," Brian said. "That's lower than last night, OK?"

Bob nodded.

"Ten seconds, Guys. Nine, eight, seven, six, five, four...." Keith looked back over his shoulder and shouted the remaining numbers. "...three, two, one!"

They vanished into the night.

Just as on the practice run, the little aircraft lurched upward with the sudden loss of weight. Keith punched the *Start* button on one of two stopwatches he Velcroed to the top of his clipboard, then pulled the throttle to idle and turned off the panel lights, leaving only the red overhead floodlight to illuminate the cockpit.

"Good luck, Guys," he told the empty cockpit.

The realization that he was alone and required to stick the plane on a darkened dirt strip in the middle of nowhere finally set in. His heart pounded from excitement and adrenalin, not fear.

They were really doing it. It wasn't a Bruce Willis movie. There were no special effects or soundtrack. Keith methodically set the GPS to display his final approach course. He calculated the size of the turns that would put him where he needed to be. Focusing on the task took his mind off the danger. He proved he could do what was needed the previous day. At least no one was shooting at him yet.

"Nine thousand," he muttered. "I'll kill the engine at two thousand feet."

Brian and Bob fell at terminal velocity, somewhere around 145 feet per second. They would reach 2,000 feet in just fifty-five seconds. Bob wasn't enjoying the ride, but he did his best to follow Brian's instructions.

The wind noise was deafening even though they wore helmets and earplugs. Brian noted they were over the drop zone and glanced at his wrist altimeter that unwound at a furious pace. Reaching down, he pulled the ripcord. The chute deployed with a loud snap, as the Kevlar shrouds strained under the weight of the two men and their gear. The pull on the harness was tremendous. Both men grunted under the strain. A moment later, they hung in the darkness.

It was quiet. Brian manipulated the risers to turn into the wind and line up with the drop zone. As the pair floated silently, the gear bag hung twenty feet below. When they approached the landing site, the bag dragged through an unseen stand of palm trees, yanking the men horizontally for a moment before returning to vertical.

Brian pulled hard to arrest their descent, but they still hit the ground hard. Again, Bob ended on top, both men on their backs. Brian silently unclipped Bob's harness and pushed him off. Bob quickly pulled the line that led to the gear bag.

"You all right?" Brian whispered.

"Yeah, I'll live. Let's not do that again, though, OK?"

"OK. You get the gear. I'll get the chute. Let's get out of the open."

They followed the plan. In less than a minute, they squatted in the ground cover at the edge of the drop-zone clearing. It was pitch black, but the NVGs made navigating as easy as if it were daylight. Wind rustled the trees, creating ambient sound that masked their movements.

"So far, so good," Bob said softly. "Move to the generators and rig that fuel tank to blow, then head to the dock and rig that, too. Disable all the boats but one if you have time. Call me on the radio and tell me which one still works. Swing past the Pier House on your way to the Great House just in case she's still in there. I'll rig the satellite uplink before I go into the Great House. If you find her first, call me on the radio. Rendezvous at the dock. I show five past the hour."

"Got it." Brian checked his watch.

Bob pulled the tactical radio from his vest and plugged in his earpiece. "One and Two are down, all OK."

"OK," Keith replied. "Three on the ground in eight minutes."

The two men divided the gear between them and blacked their faces.

"I'm on my way." Brian moved toward the generators, which he heard running in the distance.

Caretaker used a slim-jim to open the lock on the bathroom window of the Pier House and carefully climbed inside. Riley was still tied to the bed, blindfolded, her hands over her head and one foot tied to the canopy.

She heard someone moving. "Hello? Is someone there?"

Caretaker carefully peered into the room to make sure the guards were still outside. "Emily!" he hissed. "We have to go, Emily." He moved toward the bed.

"Go? Go where? Who are you? How do you know my name?" She was agitated, exhausted, and frustrated.

Caretaker moved closer. "Hush! You'll alert the guards." He removed her blindfold.

Riley struggled to focus her eyes, as Caretaker loosened the ropes that bound her feet. "Who are you, and where are we going?"

"Emily, your husband's here. He's coming for you. We must

go."

"Bob? He's here? How do you know him? How do you know my name?"

Caretaker worked as fast as his aging, arthritic fingers allowed. He shook from adrenalin and the genuine knowledge that if he was caught, he'd be killed. "I know a great many things about you, Emily. Right now, we need to get out of here." He untied her hands, and she sat on the edge of the bed, rubbing her eyes.

"Why do you keep calling me Emily? Who are you? Why should I trust you?" She was near hysteria.

"Because...." He paused. "Because, my dear, you are...." He fought for the right words. "I am...your father. You *must* trust me right now." He looked her in the eyes.

"No. My father's dead. You're full of shit. Who are you? What do you want from me?" She beat the old man's chest with both hands, as anger and tears filled her eyes. Emotionally spent, she couldn't deal with the flood of feelings overwhelming her.

"Emily, listen to me. I'm your father. Look." Reaching into his pocket, he produced a gold doubloon.

Riley gasped, her eyes widening as if she saw a ghost. Her fists stopped hitting him.

"Do you remember the last day we spent together?" he asked. "You were just a little girl. We went diving and found a gold doubloon like this one. We buried it on Sandy Cay in an old milk box. We called it your treasure box. Do you remember how we listened to Buddy Holly songs on an old cassette player in the boat? Your favorite song was *Peggy Sue.*"

She was so overwhelmed with emotion, she couldn't breathe. No one beside Bob knew about Sandy Cay, and *no one* knew about the Buddy Holly records. She forgot that detail until just then. She forced herself to focus.

"Where have you been the last thirty-eight years?" she demanded.

"That doubloon came from the wreck of the *San Salvadore.* When we got home, I got drunk and ran my mouth at the bar that night. The Columbian drug cartel got wind of it. They were powerful men. They wanted to know where I found it. If I told them, they would've killed me. If I didn't, they would've killed you, your brother, and your mother, so I staged an accident. If I was dead, they'd stop looking for me. I always planned to come back, to...."

He stared at her, tears running down his face. Riley tried to process the emotions and information suddenly thrown at her. Looking at the old man, she suddenly pulled back his shirt collar to expose his tattoo, and she realized he was, indeed, her father.

"Oh, my God, Daddy!" She wrapped her arms around the fragile old man and cried.

They embraced for a moment, then Caretaker whispered, "Emily, time is short. We must go now. Please, follow me and be quiet."

Riley stopped crying. Remembering her life was in imminent danger she released him and wiped her eyes on her sleeve before following him out the bathroom window.

Brian reached the generators and pulled a golf-ball-sized

piece of C-4 from his pack. The running machines were quite loud, and Brian didn't like being unable to hear if someone approached over the din. The smell of diesel was heavy in the air, nauseating him.

He carefully inserted a detonator and connected it to a remote trigger. Placing the package on the fuel line from the storage tank to the generators, he flipped the switch to arm the trigger. Working close while wearing NVGs was easy, but their narrow field of vision made running with them difficult.

Brian moved as quickly as he could, every sense on maximum. It reminded him of jungle training in the Marines. The heat, humidity, thick underbrush, and darkness were like a big flashback, but he wasn't nineteen anymore, and his body constantly reminded him of his age. He knew he'd be sore in the morning, but he'd worry about that later.

From the generators, it would take a few minutes to move down to the dock.

"Two thousand feet," Keith muttered. The runway was visible in the night-vision goggles, though not as well as the runway the previous night. He determined he could make the landing, so he reached up and pulled the mixture knob all the way out, killing the engine's fuel supply. The airplane became eerily quiet. He heard the electric gyros spinning, as the propeller stopped.

"Slightly high," he said, thinking that was better than the alternative. The little Maule became a glider, and he had only one shot at landing.

Keith saw sea spray breaking over the runway's approach

end, reminding him of the nearly direct crosswind. Carefully, he pulled on the lever between the seats to lower the landing flaps just ten degrees, which increased his rate of descent and lowered the nose angle, so he could see better.

"One thousand to go, still high, slightly fast." He adjusted the glide path. "Runway made." He pulled full flaps, forcing the plane to descend steeply to the runway, keeping the nose above the dirt surface and bleeding off his speed.

He touched down in the middle of the dark, deserted runway. The aircraft rolled 500 feet to assure it wouldn't be seen from the dock on the other side of the cut before he applied the brakes.

The plane stopped. Keith, pulling off his NVGs. It was so quiet the only thing he could hear was the sound of his heart pounding in his chest. He reached up to kill the master switch without thinking.

"Three is down," he said into the tactical radio. "Everything OK."

There was no response, but he knew Bob and Brian heard him. Keith unstrapped his seat belt and jumped from the plane. Going to the cargo compartment, he grabbed the two five-gallon gas cans. Walking down the length of the remaining runway, he poured gas in a straight line down the crushed-coral surface. When all the gas was gone, he jogged back to the plane, carefully placing the empty cans at the beginning of the line. He reached into the pilot's door side panel and stuffed the flare pistol into a cargo pocket on his flight suit.

Unpacking the Remington 70 from its case, he loaded a clip from the box of 7.62 ammo stashed inside, walked to the dock, and took up a position where he could cover his retreating comrades. With the rifle butt, he smashed the last dock light, set the rifle on the dock box, and peered through the scope.

He saw Brian coming down the dock to rig the boat.

"Three has Two in sight," he said softly.

Brian froze, glared at the dock across the cut, and flipped Keith the bird.

"Nice," Keith said.

Brian rigged one of the two center consoles to explode, just like he rigged the fuel tank on the generator, then he climbed off the boat and moved toward the Pier House.

"North boat rigged," Brian said into the tac radio. "South boat clear."

Bob was on the Great House's sun deck, rigging the satellite dish. He heard the transmission but didn't reply, because guards were everywhere. There was activity in the window, but he couldn't make it out clearly through the curtains.

When he finished, he climbed down, a slow, meticulous process. Once again on the ground, he walked to the front of the Great House to find a way inside.

As he turned the corner, he came face-to-face with a patrolling guard. There was no time to react. The guard leveled his weapon at Bob. Bob shot first and dropped the man.

Hadan stopped his preparations. "Go see what's going on," he told one guard, sending him down the stairs. "Leave me a weapon and go with him," he told the remaining guard.

The last guard was reluctant to leave, because he was under orders from KSM.

"I said leave me your weapon and go!"

The guard put down his AK-47, drew his pistol, and followed the first guard down the stairs.

"Put us online," Hadan told Mohesh.

"But it's not time yet. We're early." Mohesh was clearly more concerned about the single shot than Hadan. He nervously glanced at the staircase.

"Do it now!" Hadan leveled the AK-47 at the reporters.

Padma and Mohesh shrank behind the console that controlled the satellite, and Mohesh obeyed. Lights went on, and the red light on the camera showed it was operating.

Hadan sat in front of the camera to begin his dissertation.

Akshay and Rushi were on their way to the Great House from their rooms when they heard the shot and hurried toward the sound.

Riley and Caretaker came down the path passing in front of the Great House. Caretaker had no idea where Bob was, but the report from his M-4 gave him a good idea. He planned to head toward the docks and leave the island.

Brian heard the shot, too, from his location in front of Pier House. He watched a guard enter the doorway, then call for the other guard to join him. Riley wasn't there.

Moments later, the guards came out, visibly upset, shouting in their own language and rushing off.

"One bogie down," Bob said on the tac radio.

Brian made an instant call, knowing he could take down the two guards without any collateral damage. Standing, he shouted, "Hey!"

The two turned, and Brian squeezed off two rounds in quick succession, killing both of them. To ensure Riley wasn't in the Pier house, he ran in and saw the restraints on the bed, but no Riley.

"Pier House empty," he said into his radio. "Heading to Great House."

Bob waited for the guards to come downstairs. The first one met the same fate as he comrade did a minute earlier. The second guard ran down the stairs, firing his pistol. Not wanting to become drawn into a firefight inside the building, Bob backed out the door, hoping the guard would follow. He did.

"Three bogies down," Bob said.

"Plus two at Pier House," Brian added, hustling down the darkened path toward the gunfire.

Bob stepped over the dead guard sprawled across the doorway. Clearing the room ahead, he reached the staircase and took the first step, only to be met by a hail of automatic gunfire from above. The rounds penetrated the dividing wall at the top of the stairs, lodging in the back wall of the staircase.

Bob lay motionless for a moment, then silently set down his M-4. Drawing his pistol from his hip holster with one hand, he pulled a flash bang grenade from his vest with the other.

Releasing the safety on the grenade, he counted silently,

One, two, three.... He tossed the weapon over the partition wall and placed his fingers in his ears to protect them from the blast. The moment the grenade went off, he planned to race up the stairs.

A thunderous explosion sent shockwaves through Bob's body. Though his eyes were closed, he saw the flash. Arriving at the top of the stairs, he landed with his pistol out, facing the room.

Hadan sat on the floor, up against the far wall, wildly firing his AK-47. Bob shot him in the left shoulder, forcing him to drop the rifle, then scanned the room.

Padma and Mohesh cowered behind an overstuffed ottoman near the control console. The chair, lights, and camera were still in place. Grenade smoke hung in the air. It took Bob a moment to understand why the explosion was so intense. He realized the Great House was equipped with hurricane glass in the windows. Instead of breaking with the blast, they contained it. He rose slowly, his pistol trained on Hadan.

"Where is she?" He stepped toward the wounded man, who glared back without speaking.

"Kill the uplink!" Hadan shouted at Mohesh. "Kill it!"

Bob trained his gun on the terrified reporters. "Is that thing on?"

They nodded, and Mohesh moved behind the console.

"Don't touch that!" Bob snapped. "Move away from the console! Now!" He motioned with his pistol, and the two reporters scrambled toward the recliner and coffee table to hide.

Bob redirected his attention at Hadan, whom he never took his eyes off. "I said, where is she?" His tone revealed a struggle for self-control.

Hadan didn't answer, so Bob lifted the man off the floor with one hand, shoving his massive thumb into the entry wound and forcing a cry of pain from his nemesis. He dragged the tall one to the chair in front of the camera, forcing him to sit down.

"Sit." He spoke as if to a belligerent canine. From his vest, he took several plastic ties similar to the ones law enforcement used instead of handcuffs, silently securing Hadan's hands behind him to the chair frame and each ankle to a chair leg.

"I'll ask you one more time." Bob lowered his face until he spoke into Hadan's ear. "Where is she?" he asked loudly.

Hadan said nothing. Bob walked to the console and found a monitor showing what came from the camera. He turned it so he could see it more easily, then he stepped back toward Hadan.

Bob drew another pistol from his vest. "Do you know what this is?" he asked Hadan. "It's a Beretta twenty-five-caliber automatic, loaded with Glaser safety slugs. These little beauties are designed to go in and not come out."

Hadan looked at the massive American. Dressed in black, his face blackened, he cut an imposing figure even to such a hardened criminal. The Beretta was small in Bob's huge hand. He had it specially modified so his oversized index finger would fit between the trigger and trigger guard.

"So you're going to kill me!" Hadan said. "Go ahead. Seventy-two virgins and Allah await me! Kill me, if you have the guts."

Bob remained calm. "One last time. Where is she?"

Hadan just glared. Bob carefully placed the little Beretta in the back of Hadan's left knee and pulled the trigger. A muffled report sounded, followed by Hadan's scream.

Bob heard a shot fired outside, but his attention remained on his task.

Akshay ran into the courtyard in front of the Great House just as Riley and Caretaker moved toward the docks.

"Stop!" he shouted.

Riley and Caretaker turned and saw Akshay level his pistol at them.

"Run!" Caretaker said.

Akshay fired.

"No!" the old man screamed, stepping in front of his daughter. The round struck the right side of his chest. He staggered backward into Riley's arms, as she, too, cried out.

"No!"

The two collapsed to the ground.

Brian, saw the muzzle flash from Akshay's pistol, and recognized Riley's voice. Through the trees, he leveled his rifle at Akshay and fired several rounds. He dropped to the ground.

Brian ran the 100 feet to where Riley and Caretaker had collapsed. Riley sat upright with his upper body in her lap. She was crying hysterically.

"Riley!" Brian called as he looked for other guards. "Are you all right?" He crouched beside the sobbing woman. "Riley, it's Brian.

Are you OK? Talk to me."

She couldn't speak, but she nodded. They looked up toward the windows of the Great House when a grenade exploded in the second-floor room.

"Riley, we gotta go." He grabbed her shoulder, but she wrapped her arms tightly around Caretaker and kept sobbing uncontrollably.

A single shot sounded inside the house. "Riley, I'm going to get Bob. I'll be back."

She didn't seem to hear him.

Brian saw the dead guards in the doorway and knew he killed two himself. Bob reported three kills so far. The kid made six. There had to be three or four more guards somewhere.

Though he was in horrific pain, Hadan knew the cameras were rolling. "Go to hell! I'll tell you nothing!" He spat toward Bob.

"Go to hell? Gladly. I'll save you a seat." He placed the barrel on the inside of Hadan's right knee and fired again.

Hadan screamed in pain. Bob squatted beside his bound adversary. Speaking softly, as if they were having a candid conversation over a glass of cognac, Bob continued.

"You're an educated man, so let me tell you a story. Have you heard of General Black Jack Pershing?" He didn't wait for an answer. "General Pershing was an American World-War-One hero. Before the war, he was the military governor of the Philippines, which housed a large US military force. They had problems with extremist Muslim terrorist attacks on the island, so General Pershing rounded up fifty Muslim terrorists and had them tied to posts for execution by firing squad."

Hadan broke his silence. "So that's what you call this? An execution? Why don't you just go ahead and kill me now and make me a martyr for all time."

"Two coming up the stairs!" Brian called from the first floor.

"Clear!" Bob replied.

Brian took the steps two at a time. His expression when he reached the top was priceless. Bob raised his hand to stop Brian.

"Let me finish my story." Bob used the same tone an adult would use while telling a child a bedtime story. "Pershing then had his men bring in two pigs, and they slaughtered them right in front of the terrorists. You see, he knew that if a Muslim touched a pig, he would be denied entry to paradise and those seventy-two virgins. He had his soldiers soak their ammunition in the pig's blood, just as I did with the Glaser safety slugs I loaded in this Beretta." He waved the weapon in front of Hadan. "Then General Pershing executed forty-nine of the terrorists and threw their bodies into a large pit along with the entrails from the two pigs."

He calmly placed the muzzle against Hadan's left ankle and pulled the trigger. Hadan cried out in pain, panting and fighting to remain conscious. "So is that it? You will kill me and deny me paradise?" Drooling and sweating, he cried as he spoke.

"I'm not done with the story. Pershing let the fiftieth terrorist go. You know what? There wasn't another extremist Muslim terrorist attack anywhere on earth for forty-two years. How about that?"

Bob methodically moved to the other side of Hadan, placed the barrel against the man's right ankle, and fired another round.

"Bob, we got her," Brian said. "We have Riley." He wondered what was going on. "We gotta go."

Bob raised his index finger, asking Brian to wait a moment. Bob planned what he would say to Hadan for a long time, and he wanted to make his point.

"You think you're all bad ass, but I know what you really are. I spent my career chasing shitbags like you. You hide behind God and religion, but we both know you're nothing more than a gangster in a dirty turban."

Bob walked to Hadan's other side. "I guess you've outlived your usefulness to me." He placed the barrel against Hadan's forehead, as the man shook uncontrollably. If he weren't tied to the chair, he would've fallen.

"Let me know if the seventy-two virgins were worth this, won't you?"

Hadan mumbled incoherently, praying and babbling. The two men locked eyes for a moment.

Bob pulled the trigger. Padma turned away, but Mohesh was too terrified to move. It was like watching a train wreck and being unable to look away.

Click.

The sound of the hammer coming down caused Hadan to jump spasmodically in his chair. The sound and smell of his loss of control of his bodily functions echoed in the silence and permeating the air.

The gun was empty. A large yellow stain appeared in Hadan's lap. Bob slowly withdrew the pistol from Hadan's forehead, where it had been pressed hard enough to leave a mark, never taking his eyes off his adversary.

Hadan stared into space, mumbling incoherently. Bob bent over to speak softly into his ear, as Hadan sniveled, shook and stared into space, shocked to discover he was still alive.

"Oh. Oh, my," he said, with his Thurston Howell the Third voice. "You might try some Club Soda on that stain." He glanced at the urine stain in Hadan's lap, clearly visible to the camera on his bright white robe. "I hear it really works. Ta-ta!" He waved bye-bye with his pinky.

Bob stood and withdrew the remote detonator for the satellite uplink from his vest, turned to the camera, and pushed the button.

The building shook from the explosion.

Hadan, realizing he'd been humiliated on live TV, screamed with his last ounce of strength, "Noooo!"

Bob bent over to face him one last time. "Yes." He nodded in satisfaction. Looking at Padma and Mohesh, he said, "Stay," and pointed at them with his index finger.

They nodded.

"Time to go." Bob walked toward the stairs.

"Riley and the old man are outside," Brian said.

"Old man?"

"Yeah, the guy from the restaurant. Charles Hardin Holly the second."

The two men went down the stairs and out the door.

"Did you really soak those rounds in pig's blood?" Brian asked.

"No. Are you kidding? He doesn't know that, though."

"Well done. Three, we're on our way to you now. Watch our back," Brian said into his radio.

"Three's ready," Keith replied.

Bob and Brian ran to Riley still clutching the badly wounded Caretaker.

"Em! Em, are you OK?" Bob went to his knees, wrapping his arms around her.

She stopped sobbing long enough to speak. "I'm OK."

"Then leave him. We gotta go."

"No. I can't leave him."

"What?"

"He's my father."

"Huh?" Bob, wondering if the terrorists did something to her, softened his tone. "Sweetheart, your father's dead. You're obviously confused. Come on. Let's get out of here."

"Not without him." She wrapped her arms around the dying man.

Bob and Brian looked at each other in disbelief.

"All right, we'll take him, too," Bob said. "Now let's go."

Riley looked at him and stood. "It's true. He knew things only my father would know."

Bob didn't have time to argue. "I've got her. You take him," he told Brian.

Brian put Caretaker's uninjured arm around his neck and lifted him from the ground.

Keith sat on the dock at Rudder Cut. Through his scope, he saw two uniformed guards and one man in a white robe moving along the beach.

"Hey, Guys, you got a hostile headed to the beach with two guards," he said over the radio.

They were a long way off. Hitting a moving target at that range wasn't likely, but he chambered a round, anyway. He watched the three figures board a three-man jet-ski and head east across the water.

"The three hostiles are on a jet-ski headed for the ocean."

There was no reply on the radio. Keith knew they couldn't be friendly, because they went toward the ocean, not toward him. He decided to risk a shot, anyway.

Taking a wild-ass guess about windage and elevation, he pulled the trigger. The Remington gave a huge report, and, one second later, he saw the round strike the jet-ski and give a bright spark on contact. The jet-ski continued moving away.

"Oh, well." He knew they were too far away for another shot.

"One and two on the dock," Brian said. "Don't shoot!"

Keith swung the rifle around to watch through the scope. Bob, Riley, Brian, and.... Who was that?

Bob, releasing Riley, jumped into the boat. Brian was fifteen paces behind carrying Caretaker. Bob turned the starter key. The engine cranked without starting.

"Shit!" He kept trying.

Brian arrived a few moments later. "What's wrong?"

"Won't start. Use the other boat."

"Can't. I rigged it to blow."

"Shit, shit, shit!"

"There are two jet-skis over there." Brian pointed at the jet-skis parked one hundred yards away.

"Good plan. Let's go."

The four scrambled over the dock, moving toward the jet-skis.

"Can you drive?" Bob asked Riley.

"Yeah, but where are we going?"

"There." He pointed toward the dock on the Rudder Cut side.

Riley mounted the jet-ski, and Bob got on behind her.

Brian asked Caretaker, "Can you hold on to me?"

He nodded but wasn't able to speak. Brian put him on the jet-ski and climbed on in front of him.

Both machines started on the first try. A series of rounds went off behind them, and they turned to see Rushi and two guards running down the path toward them, firing.

"Go!" Bob yelled.

Riley and Brian opened the throttles. Rushi and the guards ran to the end of the dock, firing at the fading sound of the two jet-skis, as they sped into the darkness. By pure luck, one round struck Bob in the middle of his back. Fortunately, he wore a vest, and the round was only from a small-caliber handgun. The impact drove him sharply against Riley.

"Are you OK?" she shouted over the wind and engine noise.

Bob couldn't speak. The round had knocked the wind out of his lungs. He reached one hand in front of Riley and gave her a thumbs-up.

Keith, lining up a shot, squeezed the trigger. One of the guards grabbed his arm and dropped his weapon. The other two saw the muzzle flash and the wounded guard and jumped into the boat. Keith kept firing, hoping to discourage further heroics, but Rushi and the remaining guard untied the boat from the dock.

The two jet skis approached in a hurry. Keith set down the Remington and sat on the edge of the dock to help Riley off.

"Bob, you OK?" Keith asked.

"Yeah." He cautiously pulled himself off the jet ski and onto the dock. Brian was a few seconds behind them.

"Who's this?" Keith asked, as Brian cut the motor and coasted to the dock.

"Give me a hand, will ya?" Brian asked.

A moment later, all five were on the dock. The silence was suddenly broken by the sound of an outboard motor from the boat leaving the dock at Musha.

"Blow it," Bob squeaked.

"What?"

"Blow the boat."

Brian reached into his vest and retrieved the detonator, flipped up the guard, and pushed the trigger. The boat exploded in spectacular fashion, hurling flaming pieces 100 feet into the night sky. In slow motion, they fell back into the sea, burning for a moment until all the fuel was consumed, when the flames extinguished themselves.

In moments, the sea was dark and quiet again.

"What's with the old man?" Keith asked.

"He saved Riley's life," Bob replied. "He's coming with us. Let's go."

"Three unfriendlies got away on a jet-ski just before you came to the dock," Keith said. "They headed out toward the ocean."

"Nothing we can do about that. We got what we came for."

"We're taking off in that direction. Maybe we should keep an eye out for them."

Those words snapped Bob back into tactical mode. The job wasn't finished. They were still in danger.

"Point taken," Bob said.

They walked toward the plane.

"Guys, I planned for four, not five," Keith said. "It'll be tight."

"Will it fly?" Bob asked.

"Yeah, Man, it'll fly. Riley, I need you in the very back with the old man. You two are the lightest. Bob, up front. Brian, I need you sitting backward in front of the cargo door, so no one falls out."

Keith and Brian helped Riley and Caretaker into the rear of the plane, as Bob removed his vest and dragged himself into the copilot's seat. Keith ran around to the pilot's door and stopped to draw a flare gun from his cargo pocket. He aimed and fired at the two empty gas cans just fifty feet away. They ignited with a whoosh, and flame spread in a line down the runway where Keith poured gasoline.

He jumped into the open door and shouted, "Hold on!" After starting the engine, he turned on the cockpit instrument lights, brought power up to full, and released the brakes. The little plane strained under the extra weight, barely clearing the small hill at the east end of the runway.

Instantly, the windscreen went black. All that lay before them was the Atlantic Ocean. Keith started a slow turn to the left, keeping the cargo door up, and dialed Palm Beach into the GPS system.

Bob took a remote detonator from his pocket and held it up for all to see. Without a word, he pressed the button.

One thousand feet below, the fuel tanks on the generators at Musha exploded. A huge fireball lit the night sky.

"Feel better now?" Keith asked sarcastically.

Bob couldn't hear him over the roar in the cabin. Taking a headset from under the seat, he put it on. "What did you say?"

"I asked if you feel better now that you blew hell out of that little island."

"Much better."

He motioned Riley to put on a headset. Brian did, too. Riley was in the back corner of the baggage compartment, Caretaker lying on top of her. Brian faced backward, his back against Bob's, his leg blocking the open cargo door with his foot firmly against the aft bulkhead.

"Riley, how you doin' back there, Girl?" Keith tried to lighten the mood. "You need an airsick bag or something?"

"I'm OK. Nice to see you, too, Keith."

Caretaker was a mess. Bleeding profusely, he motioned Riley to lower her head, so he could whisper into her ear. She pulled off the headset.

"What's with the old man?" Keith asked.

"Riley says he's her father. Wouldn't leave without him," Bob replied.

"No shit? I thought her dad was...."

Brian tapped Bob's shoulder, and he turned. Caretaker was motionless, and Riley was crying. Bob motioned her to put her headset back on.

"I'm sorry," he said softly.

"Bob, there's a hospital in Nassau," Keith said. "I can take him there if you don't think he'll make it all the way home."

"It's not gonna matter, Guys," Brian said, his finger against Caretaker's jugular vein.

"I'm sorry, Riley," Keith said over the intercom. "He told us his name was Charles Hardin Holly the second."

Riley wiped away her tears and smiled. "Is that what he said?"

"Yeah. Why?"

"That's the real name of Buddy Holly, a musician who died in a plane crash in 1958. He was my father's favorite. We listened to Buddy Holly records all the time."

The three men looked at each other, realizing the old man had put one over on them all.

"He took a bullet for me," she said sadly. "He saved my life."

"Yes, he did," Bob said.

"Wow," Keith said. "Guys, I hate to change the subject, but we have some weather we need to fly through, so we need to lose some weight. How about we ditch some gear?"

"Bri, ditch everything we're not supposed to have," Bob said.

"Got it."

Brian and Bob spent a few minutes wriggling out of their gear and tossing it out the open cargo door."

"All the guns gone?" Bob asked.

"Yep. Ammo, too."

"All right, Guys," Keith said. "We need to fly through a small line of thunderstorms. It's nothing I can't handle, but everyone needs to find a seat belt and strap in."

Brian helped Riley attach the belt from one side to the latch on the other, then he took off his belt and lashed himself to the seat back. For the next forty-five minutes, the little plane was bumped and banged by the worst Mother Nature could dish out, but none of them cared. At least no one was shooting at them.

The open door let in a fair amount of rain, and, as they flew west, the rain became increasingly cold. On the other side of the cold front, the outside air temperature dropped twenty degrees in minutes, until it was almost freezing.

Keith turned on the cabin heater, but it was no match for the open cargo door. Though it was warmer at lower altitude, flying over the ocean at night was better performed at higher altitudes in case of emergency.

Seventy miles east of Palm Beach, they broke out into the clear sky of the winter cold front. It was beautiful. Visibility approached one hundred miles, and Keith recognized Freeport directly below.

"Bob, we're starting down soon, and we'll be arriving unannounced," Keith said. "That will cause all kinds of problems with Homeland Security."

"I got a plan for that," Bob said.

"Well, do tell." Keith sat up straighter in his seat.

"Hand me your SAT phone."

Keith reached under the seat, retrieving the SAT phone wrapped in a Zip-Loc bag. Bob gave him a look.

"You're one anal retentive motherfucker," Bob said.

Keith was glad Bob had his sense of humor back.

Bob pulled off his headset and started dialing.

Keith spoke into his radio. "Palm Beach approach, this is Maule 608. Good evening."

Keith decided it was time to make their intentions known rather than explain it to the business end of an Air Force fighter.

"Maule 608, this is Palm Beach. Go ahead."

"Palm Beach, Maule 608 is a Maule mike five, 8,500 over West End, VFR to Palm Beach, squawking one two zero zero."

"Maule 608, roger. Did you say one two zero zero?"

"Affirmative. Be advised we have a medical emergency onboard. I need medical and transport standing by."

"Maule 608, what is the nature of the medical emergency."

"Maule 608 has a gunshot victim onboard. Be advised we haven't notified Customs of our arrival."

"Maule 608, roger. Remain clear of US air space until I can

get this cleared up."

"Palm Beach, that's not gonna happen. We don't have the fuel. We're landing Palm Beach in approximately thirty-four minutes."

"Maule 608, do you wish to declare an emergency?"

"Yeah. You know what? That's a good idea. Maule 608 is declaring an emergency, five souls onboard, less than one hour's fuel, squawking 7700."

"What have you done?" Brian asked, listening to the conversation on the intercom.

"Basically, I made us their problem," Keith said. "I exercised my emergency pilot-in-command authority. It probably won't hold up in court, because we created the emergency, but at least we can discuss it on the ground."

"Great."

Bob put down the SAT phone and pulled on his headset. "What's going on?"

"I declared an emergency," Keith explained. "I expect the F-16s any minute. Who'd you call?"

"Every reporter I know. Take your time getting us to the airport. The longer we wait, the bigger the crowd."

"What'll that do for us?"

"Hopefully, it keeps us from getting an all-expenses-paid vacation to Club Fed."

"How?"

"Public opinion. Our attorney general is motivated by it. The public will see this poor woman with her dead father, rescued from the bad guys on TV. They won't be able to cover it up."

"Maule 608, Palm Beach," the air traffic controller said.

Keith held up one hand to stop Bob from talking. "Maule 608, go."

"Maul 608, contact North American Air Defense Command on guard, 121.5."

"121.5 for Maule 608." Keith frowned and looked at Bob. "I didn't expect that."

"Expect what?"

"They want us to talk to the fighter jets."

"What fighter jets?"

Keith looked out the windows of the little high-winged Maule and saw off his left wing and slightly behind him a pair of F-16s flying in formation. They suddenly turned on their running lights.

"This should be good," he muttered.

"Holy shit!" Brian said, seeing the jets, too.

"Maule 608, transmitting in the blind on 121.5 calling North American Air Defense."

"Maule 608, this is NORAD 16. We are at your seven o'clock. We've been ordered to escort you to Homestead Air Force Reserve Base. Do you copy?"

Keith spoke to Bob. "They want to take us to Homestead."

"Why?"

"Probably to get us out of the public eye. They can control the situation on the ground there. It's in the middle of nowhere."

"NORAD 16," Keith said into his mic, "this is Maule 608. Unable Homestead. We have no fuel." He released the mic key.

"Let's see what they think about that."

Thirty seconds passed.

"Maule 608, I've been advised to tell you that Homestead is not an option. It's an order. Turn your aircraft to a heading of 190 now."

"An order from whom?"

"Maule 608, be advised if you don't turn your aircraft now, the use of deadly force has been authorized."

"Holy shit!" Keith said to the others. "They're threatening to shoot us down!"

"You must be kidding," Brian said.

"NORAD 16, are you kidding?" Keith asked.

"Maule 608, negative, Sir. The use of deadly force has been authorized. Turn your aircraft now, Sir."

"Let me talk to him," Bob said.

Keith shrugged and passed him the mic. "Have at it, Dude."

"NORAD 16, this is Captain Robert Hershey, New Jersey State Police, retired. How do you copy?"

"Loud and clear, Sir. How me?"

"Loud and clear. What's your name, Airman?"

"Captain Gordon Seabrook, United States Air Force Reserve. Now, Sir, for the final time, turn your aircraft to heading 190."

"Captain Seabrook, I want you to know that I have Riley Smith Hershey and Cuyahoga County Chief of Police Brian Pysinski on board, as well as Keith Michaels, formerly USAF. Have you heard of us on the news lately?"

"Yes, Sir, I have, but I have my orders. Now, please turn your aircraft."

"Captain, I'm telling you this, so you know the names of the American citizens to whom you swore an oath to protect from threats foreign and domestic. I want you to know our names, and I'm personally asking you to notify the next of kin if, for some reason, we don't land at Palm Beach. I'm asking you, Captain Seabrook, to explain to our families why you had to shoot us down."

"Stand by."

"That was quick," Keith said. "I hope it works. We're just twenty-two miles out. Of course, if it doesn't work, we'll never know."

"Maule 608, I've been authorized to offer you one last chance to change course, then I've been instructed to fire. Do you understand?"

"Yes, Captain, I understand." Bob sighed. "You and I both know we can't make Homestead, and, in all likelihood, they'd like nothing better than to have you shoot us down. They'll defend your actions as an act of Homeland Defense, and we won't be alive to refute it. Now, Captain, I'm asking you, as one American to another, to hold your fire and escort us to Palm Beach."

"Sixteen miles," Keith said, pointing to the airport beacon visible through the windshield. "There it is."

Suddenly, the two F-16s dropped back behind the Maule.

"Shit!" Keith said.

"What?" Bob asked.

"He's in our six. He moved into firing position. Hold on!"

For the next four minutes, the Maule descended in a straight line for the beacon at Palm Beach International Airport. All those aboard expected to die. There was no panic or words, just resignation that their lives were in the hands of the Air Force pilots behind them.

Keith turned on his landing lights, ran his landing checklist, and keyed the mic. "Palm Beach Tower, Maule 608, four east landing Palm Beach, negative numbers."

"Maule 608, I've been instructed not to issue a landing clearance. Wind is two niner zero at eleven. You aren't cleared to land runway two seven right."

Keith chuckled.

"What's so funny?" Bob asked.

"The tower controller is rooting for us."

"Roger. Maule 608 is not cleared to land runway two seven right."

One mile from the threshold, Keith reduced power and dumped his flaps. The F-16s roared past on the left and right sides. When they were clear, they hit the afterburners and pulled up nearly vertical. The glow of burning kerosene trailing behind the jets looked like the tail of a satanic beast.

"Those fighter jocks just torched their careers for us," Keith said.

"Why?"

"They were ordered to shoot us down, and you talked them out of it."

It was almost three o'clock in the morning. There was no traffic on the streets surrounding the airport except for a procession of vehicles coming from all directions with blue and red lights flashing.

"They're coming for us," Bob observed.

"No shit, Captain Obvious. I can't wait to see how we talk our way out of this one." Brian laughed.

Everyone was cold, tired, and hungry. The adrenalin wore off long ago. Keith guided the little plane to a smooth touchdown in the middle of the runway.

"Maul 6o8, taxiing to the Galaxy ramp." Exhaustion sounded in his voice.

"Maule 6o8, there's a welcoming committee waiting for you. Welcome home."

"Thanks. Glad to be home."

"Nice landing," Bob said.

"Yeah. I kinda wanted to make my last landing as perfect as possible. No chance they'll ever let me fly anything again."

"We'll see about that."

As they approached the general aviation ramp, they saw police cars everywhere, and an ambulance pulling onto the tarmac. Overhead, news choppers appeared seemingly out of nowhere. As Keith taxied closer to the waiting vehicles, they saw the antennas of news trucks popping up like mushrooms after a rainstorm.

Keith methodically turned off the lights and ran the shutdown checklist. The engine shuddered to a stop. In what seemed like slow motion, Palm Beach County Sheriff vehicles of all descriptions surrounded the aircraft.

Bob pulled off his headset and jumped down from the plane. Brian stepped out the open door onto the tarmac and gently lifted Caretaker's lifeless body from Riley. Keith opened his door and walked around the back of the aircraft to help.

Keith and Brian lifted Caretaker, one man under each arm, and headed toward the ambulance. Bob extended his hand into the plane and guided Riley out. They turned toward the ambulance.

As they approached the waiting vehicle, the rest of the sheriff's cars surrounded the plane. Officers jumped out, along with EMTs, and fire-rescue personnel.

As if on cue, the crowd began applauding and cheering. It took Bob and Riley a moment to realize the applause was for them. A tall, uniformed sergeant pushed his way through the police line and walked out to meet them.

"Captain Hershey?"

Bob stopped, ready for a fight.

"I'm Patrol Sergeant Horton of the Palm Beach County Sheriff's Office." Horton was almost as imposing as Bob.

The officer extended his hand, and Bob released Riley to shake it. He realized the officer hadn't come to arrest them.

"Welcome home, Captain Hershey," Horton said. "We don't have a lot of time. I need to speak with you and Chief Pysinski for a moment."

"OK. Riley, get in the ambulance and send Brian over here."

Riley, nodding, and walked away.

"Before you say anything, Captain, you need to know whatever happened over there was on network TV. Apparently, everyone saw it."

Bob was too tired to care. "Thank you, Sergeant. I'll keep that in mind."

Brian walked over to them.

"Captain Pysinski, I presume?" Horton asked.

"Yes."

"Gentlemen, Homeland Security is on its way. They asked us to detain you until they arrived. However, my lieutenant, Lieutenant Torres, saw the TV broadcast earlier and called me to ask if I would extend you an offer. He wants you to know he'd be happy to take you into custody in the investigation of the double homicide associated with your wife's abduction. She could be considered a material witness, and therefore, we can hold y'all for up to forty-eight hours. That'll give you time to get your legal counsel in order before Homeland gets their hands on you."

Bob and Brian recognized a gift horse when they saw it. Local law enforcement would be much friendlier than Homeland Security.

"Sounds great," Bob said. "Tell your lieutenant thanks. Can you arrange for all of us to get to the hospital? We're in pretty rough shape."

"Yeah. There shouldn't be a problem with that."

"One more thing. Can you get me in front of those reporters for about sixty seconds?" Bob needed to get his story on the record before Homeland Security could stop him.

The big policeman thought for a second. Looking around to see who was there, he said, "Tell ya what. I'll have the ambulance drive around to the front of the terminal, and I'll walk you through to the other side. You can stop and say what you have to, but then you need to get into the ambulance. Will that work?"

"Yeah. That'll be perfect. Thank you."

"No problem."

CHAPTER ELEVEN

Riley and Bob walked through the terminal, while the ambulance drove to the front. They walked through the doors, into an overwhelming crush of reporters. Cameras flashed in a hail of light. Video lighting snapped on, and suddenly, the inside of the terminal was brighter than noon at the beach.

The police, led by the sergeant, herded Bob and Riley through the crowd. Reporters called questions in a cacophony so loud, it was impossible to understand them.

"Mr. Hershey! Mrs. Hershey! Robert Powell from *The New York Times!* Can you tell us what happened out there?"

Bob stopped and raised his voice to silence the crowd. "If everyone will give me a moment, I want to make a statement."

The din diminished instantly until only the sound of camera shutters was audible. Bob took a towel from the EMT who was escorting them, then slowly wiped his face and the back of his neck before placing the towel in his pocket. Riley stood beside him as if in a trance, staring into space. Wet, cold, shivering, wrapped in a blanket and covered with blood, she was quite a sight. Bob understood the impact of such an image, and took his time.

"My name is Robert Hershey. This is my wife, Riley. A little over seventy-two hours ago, she was kidnapped from a marina here in Palm Beach. Foreign terrorists took her to an island in the Bahamas and threatened her with execution. When it became obvious to me that the government," he paused to clear his throat, "my government, whose primary purpose for existence is to protect its citizens, wasn't going to take action, I took it upon myself to act. I believe I have the right to protect myself and my family from harm, and I exercised that right."

He paused and made eye contact with one of the reporters, then shifted his gaze to look into one of the cameras. "I acted alone. The other individuals involved in Riley's rescue had no idea what I intended to do. The responsibility for any consequences rests with me. You have, or will soon, see the video. I have nothing else to add. Now, we need medical attention, so if you'll excuse us...."

Bob looked at the sergeant, and the group moved toward the door, shadowed by the mass of reporters and cameramen. Like flipping a switch, the loud shouting resumed.

"Mr. Hershey! Can you tell us who else was involved?"

"Did you know you were being televised?"

"What do you think will happen to you now?"

The questions seemed endless. Riley was on the verge of shock, and Bob was exhausted. The doors to the front of the terminal opened, and the group moved toward the waiting ambulance. Half a dozen black SUVs pulled up in a hurry.

From the lead vehicle, a man emerged before it stopped and he held his ID high above his head. "I'm Special Agent Cooper," he shouted, "from Homeland Security! I'm here to take these people into custody." He walked toward Bob.

Before Bob could reply, Sergeant Horton placed himself directly in Cooper's path. Horton was easily six-foot-four-inches tall and weighed at least 250 pounds.

"These people are in the custody of the Palm Beach County Sheriff's Office."

"Not anymore." Cooper tried to sidestep around Horton, but he stepped left and blocked his path.

"This is a national security issue, Sergeant," Cooper said. "I suggest you get the hell out of my way before I have you writing parking tickets in Iraq."

That was the wrong thing to say to a man who did two tours of duty in Iraq as a Marine helicopter pilot. "Already been to Iraq, Sir. I didn't like it the first or the second time."

"Well, then, Sergeant, get out of my way."

"Can't do that, Sir. I have orders from Lieutenant Torres of the Palm Beach Sheriff's Office to transport these people to the hospital, and that's what I will do."

"These people are terrorists and have violated countless national security protocols. They're my jurisdiction. Now hand them over!" He seemed oblivious to the fact that over a dozen TV cameras were recording every word. Calling Riley a terrorist would come back to haunt him.

"Not going to happen, Sir. Now please move your vehicles,

or I'll have them moved." Horton, however, was keenly aware of the cameras.

"We'll just see about that!" Cooper pulled a cell phone from his pocket.

Horton motioned Bob and Riley into the ambulance. A moment later, Cooper snapped shut his cell phone, motioned his men to move their trucks, and walked toward his SUV. As he climbed in, he turned toward the officer and shouted loud enough for Bob to hear, "This isn't over yet!"

It was. Bob used the press to gain favorable public opinion the same way the president did during his campaign for office.

The following day, every news station on the planet carried the story. The clip of Cooper calling them terrorists ran endlessly. The public outcry of support was deafening. The domestic Muslim community, who a few hours earlier publicly cheered for the extremists, faded into silence.

Padma and Mohesh had their own stories to tell, and they became Third-World media stars. No one could or would say what happened to Hadan, but KSM escaped. Al-Qaeda purchased an old North Korean submarine from that impoverished nation, and it was fully functional, kept ready for KSM's emergency escape plan. It loitered just east of Musha the entire time, surfacing at night and remaining submerged during the day.

When the gunfire started, KSM escaped on a jet-ski. He thought he avoided detection, but a Global Hawk watched the whole thing. No one would have known about it except that an unnamed source at the CIA sent a video of the entire shootout, subsequent rescue, and escape to all network news stations.

The event paralyzed the administration. No comment followed for two days. When no charges were filed, Riley, Bob, Keith and Brian were free to go. The two F-16 pilots were asked to resign their commissions. Both were immediately and publicly offered jobs by a major US airline, and both accepted.

Brian was welcomed home as a local hero and returned to his job as chief of police. The FAA suspended Keith's pilot certificate for ninety days for violating the catch-all regulation of *careless and reckless operation of an aircraft*, but he didn't care. He decided it was time for Debbie and him to take a long trip in their motor home.

Within days, Bob was deluged with requests for media events. The state Republican Party approached him to ask if he would run for Congress for the state of New Jersey. While the attention was flattering, Bob always reminded everyone that his mission wasn't a political statement. All he did was defend his family.

It took a little longer to get the Bahamian government to agree to drop all charges and requests for Bob's extradition, but, in the end, the public pressure forced their hand. The Bahamians, embarrassed by the incident, knew no matter how much money Middle East investors spent in the Bahamas, their economy was based on American tourism. Bahamians are a laid-back people, but they aren't stupid.

The episode brought closure to Bob for that night on the New Jersey Turnpike, when he took a turn on life's road that he hadn't chosen but was, instead, chosen for him. The whole ordeal put things into proper perspective and allowed him to prioritize those things that were truly important.

Besides, he still had his bar. The Dirty Turban's walls were festooned with photos and news clippings from newspapers around the country, sent by adoring supporters of the man who stood up for his principles at great risk to himself. The Turban enjoyed a tremendous upsurge in popularity.

Bob was able to drive past *the spot* without feeling anxious anymore, but he wouldn't return to his old life just yet. There was still some unfinished business.

Riley drove the shovel into the sand, careful not to damage what she knew was waiting to be unearthed. When the tip of the shovel struck something hard, she dropped to her knees and began clearing away the sand by hand. In a few moments, the top of the treasure box she buried with her father nearly forty years earlier appeared. It was nothing more than a galvanized steel milk box, the kind milkmen used to deliver fresh milk and eggs in the '50s and '60s.

Clearing away the sand, she carefully opened the lid. Inside was the gold doubloon she and her father buried so many years ago. When she took it out, it bore identical markings to the one he gave her on Musha.

Under the priceless coin was a small plastic bag, which she also retrieved. Inside she found a faded Polaroid picture of Riley and her dad. On the back, in her handwriting, were the words, *Daddy and me, April 14, 1972.* Below that appeared the numbers *27 17 15* and *78 27 10,* followed by the name *San Salvador.*

Her eyes filled with tears, and she choked on an upwelling of emotion. It was the only photo of the two of them together that she possessed. Carefully, she reinserted the photo into the bag and placed it in her backpack. She removed her father's urn from the pack, placed it in the milk box, and remembered the day they buried the treasure.

It was a day like the present one, warm and breezy, with the smell of the ocean in the air. Wind blowing through the tops of weather-beaten pines was the only sound. Her senses went into overload. She closed the lid and pushed sand back into the hole.

When she finished, she put the stone marker back where she found it. Wiping tears from her cheeks, she paused and rose to her knees.

"Good-bye, Daddy."

Slowly, she returned to the beach where Bob waited. Visiting that spot was something Riley had to do alone so she could find closure. All Bob needed to do was be nearby.

When Riley reached him, she sobbed openly.

Bob wrapped his bear-like arms around her and whispered, "It's all right. I'm here. Go ahead and cry."

Riley looked up at him. "That night in the plane, right before he died, he whispered in my ear."

Bob let her talk, seeing her struggle to find the words.

"He said, 'Emily, I know I have no right to ask for anything, but I beg you to do this for me. Bury my ashes in the treasure box on Sandy Cay. That was the last place and last time I was ever truly happy.'"

Overwhelmed by emotion, she began crying again. "At first, I thought he asked me to do that just for him." She fought to breathe evenly. "Inside the box, I found this." She reached into her pack and took out the doubloon and the photo.

Bob studied the coin before unwrapping the photo.

"It's the only picture of the two of us that I have. I think he tried to say there was a time when we were happy, when we were a family. I think he wanted me to have it, so he sent me here to do this." She sniveled uncontrollably and was almost babbling.

"September fourteenth, 1972," Bob read. "Did you write this?"

"Yeah. That's my handwriting, but I don't remember writing those numbers. I don't know who did. Maybe he did. Anyway, I don't know what they mean, and we never went to San Salvador."

Bob's eyes grew wide. "Em," he said slowly but excitedly.

She looked up at him.

"Em, I think I know *exactly* what these numbers mean."

She stopped crying for a moment. "What?"

"These are latitude and longitude coordinates. He wanted you to have this picture, because he was trying to tell you something. He wanted to tell you where this is." He held up the doubloon.

Riley took a moment to ingest the information. "*San Salvador*. It's not a place. It's the name of a ship!" She smiled through her tears, then began to laugh.

"Come on," Bob said. "Let's go home."

MORE BOOKS FROM PENNINGTON PUBLISHERS

James Gardner's adventure-thriller introduces Rigby Croxford, ex-military, native of Africa who finds that life now takes him on hard twists and deadly turns created by the minds of desperate people in desperate situations. **Money, avarice, lust, passion**, romance and deep-seated, disturbed thinking propel him through moment-by-moment, jaw-dropping action. The most deadly animals are *other men*

PENNINGTON PUBLISHERS

THE ZAMBEZI VENDETTA

" *His powerful writing illuminates The Dark Continent.* "

—Nelson DeMille, New York Times Best-Selling Author

DARK CONTINENT CHRONICLES BOOK II

" *Gardner's story telling approach follows in the path of Dashiell Hammett: 'Life is disposable; the Land beautiful and the search is fatal.* "

—James Edstrom, Times Square Gossip

JAMES GARDNER

For Rigby Croxford fans!
Rigby Croxford returns in this spine-chilling saga about the harrowing escape attempt by six American tourists caught in the middle of a bloody civil war in Africa. They are left with no choice but to brave the dark and deadly Zambezi River.

BOOKS FROM OUR FRIENDS AT MUSE HOUSE PRESS

FIXED STARS RISE

CHARLES T. LAFFODAY

ꟽꞪꝐ
muse house press

Author Charles T. Laffoday weaves a psychedelic tale of our culture's history with characters that are at once familiar and strange. They turn out to be the guardians or keepers of our culture and of truly unique ideas. More importantly, these guardians are all around us now...

www.ingramcontent.com/pod-product-compliance
Lightning Source LLC
Chambersburg PA
CBHW050034180626
46810CB00002B/707